In The Garden Room

In The Garden Room

TANYA EBY

Blunder Woman Productions
Grand Rapids

Illustration by Kim Hindman - 10digitpress

Cover Design by Beetiful Book Covers

Weed, Clarence Moores. Nature Biographies; *The Lives Of Some Every-day Butterflies;
Moths; Grasshoppers and Flies.* New York: Doubleday, Page & Co, 1903

ISBN: 978-0-9860133-8-6

ACKNOWLEDGEMENTS

There are so many people I'd like to thank. First, to my husband, David Kolenda for putting up with me in general and listening to me brainstorm and complain.

Then to Erin Augustine who became my online writing partner and pen pal. I wouldn't have finished this book without her holding me accountable for new pages every couple of weeks.

Christine Allen-Riley for being an awesome proofer/editor and for making some hard suggestions that turned out to be right.

And…to my Beta Readers…who offered to read the rough draft of this novel and give their feedback and asked for nothing in return. Your effort and energy meant the world to me. My Beta Readers: Patrick Callahan, Colleen Corbin, Gina Dawe-Weaver, Robert Kostic, and Ken Schmidt.

And last, but not least, the fabulous Kim Hindman, a dear friend, but also the artist of the print featured here in this book. Follow her work at www.facebook.com/10digitpress.

She had grown tremendously fond of the insects, of how their short lives revolved wholly around the process of change.

— "Sin in the Second City", Karen Abbott

There gathered, before the matinee and afterwards, not only all the pretty women who love a showy parade, but the men who love to gaze upon and admire them.

— "Sister Carrie", Theodore Dreiser

In The Garden Room

AFTER

DECEMBER
1910
CHICAGO

LILLIAN

Papa says we have to move the body and come up with a story before anyone finds out. I find that very odd. Not the story part, I am used to stories, but the part about the body. Just an hour ago, that body was Mother, but now she's gone. Her soul hissed out like steam from a kettle. I cross to the object that was Mother but now is The Body. Father says hurry, and I do. "The police will be here soon, and we must be ready," he says. He does not know that the police only come to the Packinghouse District to drink and to open their trousers.

There isn't time for me to see the room through my father's eyes, but I do anyway. It is easier to see the room than it is to look at the deep red staining my hands and dress. The drops on the floor that start small and blossom, like crimson fireworks. I don't look at her boots with the many small buttons. At her torn stockings and too-short skirt. At her sad, exposed bosoms, like white dough gone too long to rise. I don't look at her face and her open eyes, and the red blooming along her front. I look at the room while Papa scrubs my hands with a stiff brush and cold water.

There is my blanket in the corner. The corner where I would curl up and read and stare at the postcard of home and the cherry trees in bloom. There is the iron bed with the mattress that smelled of damp earth and the lake. The wallpaper is curling in the upper right corner as if it's a snake shedding its skin. There are playbills nailed to the walls. The places Mother went to, maybe, in the beginning. The places she dreamed of going later. The places she'll never go to now.

My hands burn.

"Let's get you changed and then I'll take you out of here. There's nothing left to do now. Don't you have anything here to change into?" he says. His words are thick and slow in my head.

I cannot speak. I am metamorphosing like the bugs in the biology book I used to read. My words are stones in my throat. I shake my head.

"Is this all you have here?" he asks and I can hear the sorrow clinging to him. This is an empty room. There is nothing of me here, not even Mother. "She left home for…" Now, Papa has no words. Maybe he is metamorphosing, too.

He squeezes my hands in his. He has fisherman hands. Firm and rough and warm, but I am not afraid of his hands. He is not like the other men. Even now, he still thinks I am just a girl.

I point to the dresses she has hanging on the door. There are two. One looks like a costume, and I suppose it is; it is meant to be taken off quickly. He grabs the light blue one, the summer dress. This was the dress she wore when she took me from him. It is stained and torn, the hem thick with mud and horse dung. Once, it was the color of the Michigan sky over the bay, its ruffles like whitecaps surfacing. The blue is more grey now, and it smells of loss.

"Put this on," he says. "I will tend to…" He turns away from me, for propriety, I guess, and I try to stop the giggle from bubbling. He thinks there are still things left for me to hide.

I dress. What I'm wearing now is no better than a sack, and it pools at my feet. I step out of it, and into the dress that once clung to my mother's curves. The bustle is long gone now, and the back of the dress floats on me. I breathe with relief. It does not fit me. Her curves are in the wrong places, so maybe there is hope that I will not grow into her shape.

"Come on, my Lil," Papa whispers. "It's over, now. It's over. It's time for us to go."

Mother and I have lived here for two seasons, nearly three. I was a child when we first arrived and I am leaving transformed. Worse than becoming a woman, I have become a monster. I know it is worse because I am glad of it. In the blue stained dress, I am a demon, and I am smiling because we are free of her.

PART ONE

BEFORE

JULY

1910

TRAVERSE CITY, MICHIGAN

❧ 1 ❧

Cora March watched her daughter pitting cherries for the pies. The apron Lillian had sloppily tied around her neck was stained and splattered with cherry bits, and her brown braids were loose and wispy. The worst was Lillian's hands. They were stained a bright red, the juice bleeding from her fingertips clear across her palms. It would mean an hour of scrubbing her small hands with the special soap she'd made to get the stink of fish off her husband. It meant more work for her. Always, everything, more work for her.

Still, they'd arrive to the picnic tomorrow with a beautiful pie (leaving an equally beautiful pie with the Millikens as payment), and Cora would wear her blue dress and a flower in her hair and she would dance and sing and laugh, again. She could feel the oncoming picnic like the sun on her shoulders, heating her through. She felt like laughing now, even though Lillian was pitting the cherries all wrong.

"You've put too many in!" Cora said. "You've got them all jammed in there."

Lillian stirred the stuck cherries in the pitter's shoot with the handle of a wooden spoon, trying to break things up. (She'd stain the handle, too; only there'd be no getting that out with soap.) Cora watched her turn the crank, and a pulverized cherry spat out of the metal mouth. It was such a beastly contraption, chewing and spitting that way. She'd rather pit cherries by smashing them with a knife and scooping out the pit, but the pitter was the way all the women were doing it now. And she had to be like all the other women, didn't she? There was no choice in that. Not like men. They could be whomever they wanted.

"It's not clogged anymore," Lillian said with a hint of triumph in her voice.

Her voice ran like a ragged fingernail against Cora's spine. She looked at the bowl of pitted cherries and felt heat in her cheeks. The cherries were vile. Pulverized. Mashed up bits of goo. "Lillian!" she said. "You're ruining them! I want these pies to be perfect, and they won't be like that." She gestured to the bowl and it's gelatinous contents.

"But the cherries are *inside*, Mother. No one's going to see the *inside* of the pie."

Cora's jaw clenched, tight with the words she wasn't saying. It was the *inside* that mattered most. Lillian was just too young to know this yet, but she'd learn. She took a deep breath. "When you're done with that, I'll show you how to roll out the crust."

"I know how to roll the crust. Can't you do it? I'd like to go outside for a while."

Outside. Outside. Always outside. Sometimes Cora thought Lillian wasn't a girl at all, but some kind of farm animal. Where was the daughter she'd envisioned? The one who was a proper lady and quiet and beautiful and stayed out of her way?

What was the point? Why put so much effort into trying to train her right. Nothing in her life was the way she'd dreamed. Why should it be different for her daughter?

Cora turned her back to her and marched across the small kitchen to sit at the window. The kitchen was the only room in the tiny house that had any kind of a view. *We should have a view,* she thought. She looked out the window, searching past the trees and trying to see that thin strip of blue beyond the trees where the bay stretched. Did she see a line of blue? It might be the bay, or just the horizon. When she looked out, sometimes she could picture she had the daughter she'd dreamed about. And the husband. And the life.

Her hand toyed with the cameo at her throat. Her lips stretched in a thin smile. If she was being honest, and she was always honest, she'd admit that the life she should have had didn't include a husband and a daughter at all. It had lights and stage dust and ghost lamps and applause. Her intended life, the life she deserved, had real passion. What she was living now was just a rehearsal.

The rehearsal was this: They lived in a small cottage on the Milliken family's property, next to the carriage house, so close, in fact, the stench of hay and horse dung lingered thick in the summer heat. While Lillian was in school, Cora walked down the twisting path and through the back of the Milliken's twelve-bedroom home with the wraparound porch that looked out at the bay. The family would sit and fan themselves and drink fresh lemonade while inside she (and two other women) sweated and scrubbed the floors and cleaned and swept the attic and checked for bats. There were always bats. The attic was a hive of them. At night, they flew in under the roof's shingles. Bat guano slipped down the attic walls and Cora cleaned it. That's who she was. A fisherman's wife. A mother. A cleaner of bat shit. No applause for that. No stage light and magic with bat droppings in your hair.

She tried to imagine that some prince would rescue her, but her back ached too much to be fully swept into that idea. When she walked back up the path, Lillian would be waiting for her, and later in the evening, John would come home, fresh from his work at the fishery where he gutted salmon and whitefish. This was her life. Work and stench and mothering. She could barely stomach it.

"We'll buy a cherry orchard," he'd said once. "I'll work enough and buy a plot of land up near Empire. We'll have a view of the bay and the cherry trees will stretch out for miles. We'll be rich."

"And I'll wear silk and organza," she'd said. She held the word out 'organza' because it was so beautiful and musical and because she'd believed it.

"You won't have to wear anything at all," he'd said, and he'd kissed her, his lips firm and dry.

That was when they were courting, and life was bright and tremulous, and John was interesting. Twelve years had passed, and she'd never worn anything but cotton. And he smelled of day old fish. And the cherries they had were the ones from the back of the Milliken's yard. The trees were an experiment, started to see if cherries would work in the climate. Mr. Milliken was sure they would grow, and they had, and he bought acres and acres of hilly land and planted an orchard as wide as the bay. Cora could pick as many cherries as she wanted, Mrs. Milliken said, as long as she left a pie or two in their kitchen. Nothing in life was free. You had to give something to get something, and that just grated on her, too.

Lillian screamed something, jerking Cora from her thoughts. "Papa!" she cried, and then she was off, stained hands outspread, braids flapping, cherry smeared apron bouncing. John scooped up Lillian and hugged her close to him, her long legs dangling. He didn't seem to think twice about holding her like that, not caring that the girl wasn't an infant anymore. She was eleven, and though she was small for her age, it wasn't proper for him to treat her so. When, though, were men ever proper? They were beasts.

Cora stood, moving from the window, and smoothed the front of her dress. She tried not to notice that her hands were stained, too, though from work and not from fruit.

She watched John and Lillian from the doorway. John put Lillian down and held something up above her head. A book of some kind.

Another book. Lillian jumped to snatch it with her red hands, and John lifted it just out of her reach. Get used to that, Cora thought. That was life right there…what you wanted was always just out of reach.

Finally, he lowered it enough that Lillian could grab it from him. She squealed and kissed him and took off running, no doubt to the orchard and her secret hiding place that was no secret at all. Lillian could do whatever she wanted it seemed, and it wasn't fair. "Lillian!" Cora cried, annoyed. "The pies!"

"Later, Mother! It's a book on biology!" she cried, and then she disappeared into the woods.

John approached. Cora was blocking the door. "Cora," he said in greeting.

"John," she replied. They were so formal. It was like speaking in a foreign language. "You stink," she said.

He sighed, which was his language for 'not this again'.

"We have the picnic," she said. "It's tomorrow at lunch. You'll have to bathe, tonight," she continued as if she was his mother. "And wear a clean shirt."

He stomped into the kitchen—he always stomped, incapable of walking any other way—took off his boots, and collapsed onto the chair. Bits of fish scale caught the light and he glimmered for a moment. It wasn't a real glimmer. She knew that, now.

"I'm working tomorrow," he said.

"Working?" Her mouth was small, so small it was hard to talk to him, to get the words out.

He reached into his pocket and pulled out two coins. "It's all I have left this week. Put it in the can."

Cora snatched it, ran to the shelf, stood on the tips of her toes, and dropped the two coins into the can. It made a hollow clunk sound. "Wonderful. At this rate, we'll have a cherry orchard when we're in our nineties. Two whole trees by then. I'll wear organza in my coffin."

"Not this," he sighed. "Not today."

"There. Is. A. Picnic. Tomorrow," she said. She'd been looking forward to it all year. It was the Second Annual Cherry Celebration. Last year, she'd missed it, and she refused to be left out this year. She was still young and deserved to enjoy herself.

"Then take Lillian," he said. "I'll work, and I can join you when I'm done."

"Not…"

"I'll change first," he said. "Cora…please."

He must think she was disappointed he couldn't go, so she tucked her smile away. Foolish, again. "All right," she said, and joy swept through her. She began to spin around the kitchen. "There will be dancing and games…" she hummed a tune for a moment. "There's a pie contest."

"I'm sure you'll win."

"I have talents," she said, and he nodded. He seemed angry with her, or defeated, and she didn't want him to change his mind. The picnic was everything to her. It was the one hope of something fun and real and alive. She sat on his lap, ignoring the fish scales and the stink. "Johnny," she said in the pouty way he liked. She kissed her fingertip then traced it along his beard-roughened jaw. His lips twitched. She breathed deep, and then he was on her, fish-mouth flexing and gasping on her, big man hands pushing aside her layers of cloth until he could find her center.

He'd never find her center.

He had no clue where she hid.

2

Lillian's mother wore her best dress, the blue one, with the tiny buttons at the collar. Her gloves were white and too hot for this weather, but still, they made her mother look so dignified. Lillian wore her brown dress, the one she wore to school. Mother said she needn't dress up for the picnic. Lillian didn't understand that, as her mother was gussied up like she was going to get married. Still, it made Lillian proud to walk next to her pretty mother.

It was the Second Annual Cherry Social at the small Traverse City Green, and the bay shore was flooded with families, horses and carriages and the shout of barkers trying to sell their wares. Women arrived wearing their best church outfits and carrying umbrellas to shield their delicate skin from the sun. Men wore wool pants, starched shirts, and suspenders, even though it was hot. Children ran figure eights around the adults, seemingly unaffected by the heat. Pastor Tom served fresh lemonade on the lawn with a sign that read DONATIONS FOR THE HUNGRY. He'd give you a cup of fresh squeezed lemonade for one penny; the line from the bible came free.

Lillian wished he'd keep the line to himself and just give her the lemonade.

The town was transformed into a carnival of color and laughter, and Lillian thought it was the most magical thing she'd ever experienced, magical enough to tear her away from reading the new book her father had bought for her about the life cycle of insects. Lillian was going to be a scientist, and she read every book she could that explained how life worked, even the bible—but that was more because she had to than because she wanted to.

"Hurry," Mother said. "I want to enter this pie into the contest before it gets so hot that the whole thing wilts."

Lillian laughed. Pies didn't wilt. But she was not to disagree with Mother, ever, and certainly not in public. A good daughter was dutiful and quiet. A smart daughter thought naughty things to herself and kept them locked away. Lillian, at eleven, was very smart.

She gulped the lemonade, though the tartness brought tears to her eyes. When Pastor Tom said, "May the God of hope fill you with all joy and peace as you trust in him, so that you may overflow with hope by the power of the Holy Spirit," Lillian thanked him, but secretly thought she would rather be filled with cotton candy. She'd heard there was a cotton candy machine somewhere at the fair this, year. All the kids at school were talking about it. Eleanor had been to the World's Fair in 1904 and told her cotton candy tasted like "wishes come true". Lillian had laughed at that. Wishes didn't have a taste.

"Lillian," her mother repeated, this time with that edge to her voice. "The pie."

"I can take it for you, Mother," she said.

"I don't want to risk you dropping it."

They walked to the tent where women were dropping off pies for judging. The dresses swished against their legs. Lillian's heels sunk into the grass. There was a line to sign up for the contest. Mother held the pie before her like it was a newborn infant about to take its first breath. But it was just a pie. And the top was collapsing.

"Mother, look," Lillian said, nodding to Mrs. Master's pie. Mrs. Master was short and blonde and plump and beautiful. She was only five years older than Lillian, but already she wore her hair up and had been married for two months. "Her pie looks like a painting," Lillian breathed.

"And it probably tastes like one, too," she huffed.

Lillian was bored. She wanted to find some of her friends and run off and join them, but she remained near her mother. Until Cora told her she could go, she'd have to stay close. A few paces away from them, a group of older girls stood huddled over a newspaper, giggling. "And here's another one," Amelia Knaggs said, pointing to something in the newspaper. Amelia, too, was only a few years older than Lillian, but her parents were poor. She was sure Amelia wouldn't wear her hair up and be married anytime soon, unless some man took pity on her. Amelia now read aloud: "Seeking young ladies for important clerical work in support of executives. No experience required." The girls laughed again.

"That'll be perfect for you, Amelia," one of the other girls said. "You don't have experience in anything,"

"Oh, she has experience," her mother muttered. "Just not the kind she could get paid for." Lillian didn't know what she meant.

"Where are those jobs they're reading about, Mother?" Lillian asked. When she finished school, she didn't want to do what her mother did and get married and have children. Lillian planned to see the world, study, go to college. But she'd need money to do that. "I'm sure they're talking about Chicago," her mother said. "It's my turn, now."

At first, Lillian thought she meant it was her mother's turn for Chicago, but that didn't make sense. They lived here. Then they stepped forward in line, and Lillian realized her mother had only been talking about registering the pie.

A band started playing, and the girls ran off. When her mother finished giving her name and collecting her number for the pie, she turned quickly, avoiding Pastor Tom and his tart lemonade. Lillian followed her. Cora quietly scooped up the abandoned newspaper, folded it, and put it in the picnic basket.

"Litter," she said.

෩෩෩

Cora looped her arm through the picnic basket and smiled. The smile was false, like wearing a dress that wasn't yours and dug into your waist. She'd wanted this picnic to be so different. She wanted to dance and swirl around and laugh, again. She wanted it to be like when she was courting.

The group of young girls who were reading the paper angered her. They had so much ahead of them. So much that was still unknown. What did Cora have? A husband who smelled of fish, a daughter who read books about bugs, and hands that were starting to callus.

Lillian tugged on her arm, which was already weighted down by the basket.

"Can I go off with Patricia and play? Other girls are playing, Mother. Can't I?" Her daughter's voice was sharpened to a point with need. Cora had imagined they both would sit elegantly under a tree and the townsfolk would admire Cora from a distance. They would walk by and tip their hats. But no one noticed her.

"Go on, then," Cora said, and Lillian took off running.

Cora looked for a place to sit, but the ground was soggy.

"Miss," a voice said. It was young sounding, and male. "There's a bale of hay if you don't mind sharing it with a stranger." His voice was warm honey.

Cora turned to look at a man who must have been in his early twenties. His face flushed. "Ma'am, I mean," he corrected himself.

She realized from the back, he'd thought she was still a girl. The thought depressed her.

"I would like to sit, thank you, sir," Cora said, and held out her hand for his. He took it, and his grip was firm but trembled slightly. She smiled liking that she could still affect a man so. She gave him the slightest squeeze, nothing that anyone would notice if they were looking, and they were always looking.

He led her to a bale of hay set up around the green. They had a view of the water and a sack race was going on. Cora could see Lillian wiggling into a sack. If it weren't for her long braids, the girl easily might be mistaken for a boy. Cora hoped she wouldn't come running back to them anytime soon. It had been a long time since Cora had sat with a young man.

The air was hot against her skin and carried the faint scent of fish. She hoped it was from the bay and not from the fishery where John worked. Her husband had infected every part of her, even the scent of her clothes.

"Are you new in town?" she asked and opened her basket. She offered him a slice of bread and strawberry preserves. His eyes sparked.

"We're on shore leave," he said. "My buddies are over there." He nodded and Cora could see the group of sailors talking to the young girls.

"Don't you want to join them?" she asked.

"Why would I? They're just messing around. Besides, they're missing out." He looked into her eyes. His eyes were the deep brown of fertile earth.

"Missing out? On bread?"

"And its sweet companion …" he said and paused with meaning, she thought. "…the jam," he added.

Cora felt the heat rise to her cheeks. She imagined straddling him, biting his lip. Running her tongue across his still smooth cheek. He'd have a full beard someday, but probably not for another few years. Really, he was just a boy.

Once, she had been just a girl.

She again felt the blush painting her cheeks.

"This seems like a nice place," he said, not looking at her now but at the fair going on around them. "I live in the city. Such a different world just over the lake."

"Chicago?" she asked. "I seem to be hearing a lot about Chicago these days."

"Sure you would. Best place on earth, next to here of course. When we're done with this tour, I'm giving up my sea legs. I've had enough of shipping trees."

"Trees?"

"Christmas trees. You believe that? The Germans are crazy for them. We run all up and down Michigan, shipping them over to Chicago. Course, in the summer months, we ship other things. A big shipment of cherries this year. Cherries. Of all things. I'm sure this isn't interesting to you."

"Oh, I don't know," she said. Everything outside of her life was interesting to her. "If you're not sailing anymore, what will you do?"

This time he turned to her. "My uncle owns a theater, right down by the water. I'm investing. I'm going to be his partner."

Cora couldn't breathe for a moment. If only she were ten years younger. She looked at the basket at her feet. The bread and jam. The apples for later. Someone was calling out and selling fresh peanuts. Her daughter jumped wildly in her sack, hardly moving at all, like she was some beached fish. This day, today, the sun hot on her face, the sweat tickling between her breasts, would be her best day all year, maybe for the next ten years. She could feel her spirit drying up.

"You ought to come and see me," he said softly, and then quickly followed it with, "With your family, I mean. I assume you have a husband and children?"

She thought she could feel the touch of his leg against her own, their heat burning through the fabric of their clothes.

"I do," she said. "A husband. A daughter. That one," she said, and pointed to Lillian who was spastically jumping. "But they would never go to Chicago."

"You could always come on your own," he said softly. There was a slight pause as if he were studying her reaction. Cora held her breath. "I don't mean to offend," he said, his words hushed.

She turned and looked at him, straight in the eyes, neighbors watching be damned. He had a tiny scar that cut through his eyebrow. His Adam's apple was sharp in his throat. "You don't offend," she said. They held the stare a beat.

"Mother! Mother!" Lillian came running across the green, her shouts like a thunderclap, waving a ribbon in her hand. "Second place!"

The man looked at her daughter running, a slight grin tilting his lips. "Well, then," he said and stood. "It was a pleasure to meet you, Miss…Mrs…"

"My name is Cora," she said and held out her gloved hand. He took it and kissed the top of it. One of his fingers dipped beneath the fabric of her glove so his skin touched hers.

"I'm Ezekiel. Zeke. I'll be on my way, now. Here's my card. You ever make it to Chicago, you look me up. Maybe there's a place for you at the theater. I'll be there in just two days. Two more days," he said, as if the idea of just two days were the most wonderful invention.

He handed her his card and right before Lillian barreled up to her, he whispered, "You're the prettiest girl here, Mrs. or not. If you do come, bring your girl, too. We have lots of jobs opening up." He tipped his hat to her and turned away. Cora held the card in her hand, the light touch of paper in her hand the only thing to prove to herself that magic existed in this world.

❧❧❧

Lillian stopped short of her mother. A man was holding her hand. He leaned to kiss it. Lillian felt her cheeks burn, but then the man let go of her mother and walked away. For a moment, he looked back at Lillian, and then he winked.

The ribbon in her hand was floppy with the sweat of her hand. Her mother looked at her, her face bright, and Lillian knew. Something had just shifted within her mother, something important, something dangerous. Lillian walked slowly toward her. "Mother?" she asked. "Are you okay?"

She beamed at Lillian. "I'm wonderful. I'm just wonderful!" Her words were buoyant, but Lillian felt a sinking in her stomach. She loved when her mother was happy, but it was what came after that happiness that she feared. She would tell her father. He would know what to do.

"Let's go look at the pies! Maybe I have a ribbon, too."

Lillian prayed that her mother was just "overflowing with hope by the power of the Holy Spirit," like Pastor Tom had said when he'd given her lemonade, but Lillian worried her mother overflowed with the spirit of something else.

❧ 3 ❧

The day was magic, Lillian thought. Not *magical*. Not *filled with magic*. No. The day, in its very essence was magic, itself. Lillian and her mother walked all through the fair together. They ate cotton candy, so light it was like the fluff of a cottonwood tree, but infinitely sweeter. There were food booths with ice cream; women churning the wooden cranks of ice cream makers, their men carrying in the ice and salt and dropping it at their boots. Another booth had funnel cakes and grilled sausages and peppers. There was rock candy and doughnuts piled high on long rods. Pies and cakes in stacks, starting to drip in the heat. Buckets, heaping full with black cherries, ripe for eating.

Lillian had never seen such abundance, and her mother reached into her purse and bought it all, anything Lillian wanted. She didn't know where the money had come from for all of this, and her mother didn't say. Perhaps the money materialized, as money was wont to do when under magical influences.

The sun was full and bright in the cloud-free sky. The fair had been set up just outside of Main Street, by the Grand Traverse Bay. Carriages and horses lined the gravel road. On the small beach, a few women sitting under umbrellas watched their children splash in the water. The fair itself was set up on the Common, an area of grass unmarred by sand and on a slight hill that flattened at the top. The grass had never been greener, and the gentle lapping of the bay just before them added a rhythm of leisure to the fair. Even when the band stopped playing—its music off-key and tinny—the bay continued its gentle lap, like a kitten at a bowl of milk.

Lillian's mother had never looked so beautiful. She seemed to glow from within, and pulled Lillian by the hand to every little booth to toss rings on bottles, or throw balls through hoops. Mother was terrible at these games but somehow managed to win a rose from an olive-skinned man with a thick mustache that hid his lips. "A rose for a rose," he said, his words pronounced with a strange lilt to them. Her mother giggled.

When the sun finally began to set and the air cooled, Lillian felt the gentle tug of sleep. "I'm tired, Mama," she said, as if she were still four. She hadn't called her "Mama" in such a long time it felt like someone else's name.

"But there is still dancing! And the results of the pie contest! And…" Her mother's words slipped into the bay. She released Lillian's hand as if her hand had become a spider.

Her mother stared and Lillian saw that her father was approaching. He must have come straight from the fishery, in his stained shirt and pants. His cap was askew and matched the wide smile across his face. Lillian ran to him, and he grabbed her in his arms and swung her up into the air. He smelled like home to her: that scent of the bay, and earth, and sweat.

Lillian expected her mother to run to him, too, for him to sweep both of them into his strong arms. She thought he could perhaps lift his mother into the air too and she would laugh and ask him to put her down. But Lillian's mother did not run to him. She simply stood, staunch as an elm tree. Papa removed his hat.

"Cora," he said. "I'm sorry I'm late, but I thought…" He paused. Papa was never very good with finding the right words for things. "There's music," he said at last. "There's still time for a dance." Papa was smiling, and Lillian could picture what he must have looked like when they were courting.

It had been such a good day. Her mother had been so happy. But now everything tilted, the way it did when the water was too rough, and it was hard for a boat to right itself.

Her mother stared at Papa. "Couldn't you change?" she asked, so softly it was barely audible, but Lillian felt the vibration of the words in the pit of her stomach.

"No time for that," Papa said, still sounding happy. "Time to dance!"

He grabbed her mother by the hand and tugged at her, trying to lead her to the green square where the crowd was gathering, couples poised in each other's arms, waiting for the music to start.

Lillian knew that there would be no dancing. There was no magic left in the day. They had used it all up. Papa had done the wrong thing, said the wrong combination of words, though with Mother, it was hard to know what was right. If there even was a right.

All of the food she'd eaten, the lemonade, the cotton candy, the fluffy and crisp funnel cake dusted with too much sugar, rose up in her throat. Lillian turned and ran, looking for a dark corner where she could be sick.

When she was done, she felt the strong, warm hand of her father, resting on the blades of her back. "It's all right," he said. "It's been a long day. Let's go home. There will be time for dancing another day. Hop on," he said and squatted so she could climb on his back. She wrapped her gangly limbs around him and held on.

Lillian snuggled her face into the hollow of his neck. His jostling nearly rocked her to sleep. She struggled to stay awake. For a moment, she looked back and she saw her mother walking behind them, her face pinched and angry. There would not be another time for dancing, not here, with the bay cooing to them, not with the sky darkening, not with everything familiar wrapped around her like a blanket, and Lillian would never know the winner of the pie contest.

❧❧❧

The black heat coiled first in Cora's feet then moved up her legs. It swirled around her thighs and seeped into her gut. The heat curled into fists in her chest, pummeling her from the inside.

As they walked home, she thanked God that it was dark and no one would see the state of her husband. His smell was bad enough. You couldn't miss his stench. How could he come to the fair smelling like that, when she had asked him not to?

He carried Lillian like she was a babe, when their daughter was closer to being a woman. Really, the way he treated her. It wasn't natural. How he hugged her so much, how his hand lingered on the blades of her back. Was every man just waiting to consume, even a father? What must everyone think of them? She felt their stares and pointing fingers from every shadow. How they judged. How they teased. Cora had wanted just one pure day. One day where she could be someone else. Where she wasn't his wife, and she didn't work for a rich family on the bay, and she had all the money she could spend, and where a man would look at her and see her for the beauty she was. One. Perfect. Blemish-free. Day. And she'd almost had it. But now, she felt the familiar rush of anger wash over her, sucking all other feelings into an undertow.

That boy...that man...Ezekiel...had looked at her as if she were worth something. As if he saw her as being a whole person and worthy of interest. "Come to Chicago" he'd said. He'd have a place for her at the theater. A job, maybe. Maybe he could get her into a play. Cora would heighten her beauty with rouge and stage-lights. She would have an entire audience looking at her with awe. They would whisper from the shadows, too, but there would be no taunts, then. "What a beauty!" They would say. "What a talent!" The applause would fall on her shoulders like starlight.

The black heat in her chest slithered up her throat, choking her, and finally, writhed in her mind, swirling.

She had the power to change her life.

She deserved to change her life. Her husband, John, the poor fisherman, had filled her head with falsehoods. Lies that quivered like maggots. They would never own a cherry farm. She would never wear silk or organza. Her hands would callus and blossom with brown spots like decomposing fruit.

"Come to Chicago," Ezekiel had said. His card was tucked into her glove. She could feel him there. "Bring your daughter," he'd said. She would so like to start over without Lillian, without that constant weight tugging at her, but Ezekiel had looked at her daughter kindly, and what would that say about her as a woman if she left her daughter behind? Maybe she could tell people they were sisters. She would be an actress and the world would believe anything she told them. She could start now. John was always a willing audience.

An hour later, her legs tired from the long walk home, they turned the corner past the Milliken's giant house. She could hear bats' wings fluttering above her. Their small house waited for them, tucked into the shadow of the Milliken house, the stench of horse dung heavy in the air. All of this would be a memory soon.

The black heat in her mind shifted, and took the shape of plans. One more night. One more sleep here, in this place, as this person, and then tomorrow, she could start anew.

She waited for John to tuck Lillian in. She would give him that. The fool was so sentimental. "Are you ready for bed?" he asked softly. She wasn't sure if that was an invitation for her to do her wifely duty, or if he was too tired and wanted sleep. She didn't care either way. Every step, every action, every breath, was one moment closer to being free from him and this world that suffocated her.

"I am ready," she said, and smiled in the dark.

Cora thought she would leave in the morning, but it would take a few more weeks before the opportunity sprouted, suddenly, like the coil of a fresh fern in the woods unfurling at long last.

⁂

Zeke knew women. He knew them inside and out. And shouldn't he? Wasn't he raised in The Garden Room, a place where women, like roses, were plucked over and over again by the men who could afford them. Women, like flowers, were all beautiful and horrible at the same time. Tender, fragile, desperate. Some were happy enough in their tiny lives of church works and mothering. But then there were others. The white lilies with a blush of pink, their soft legs, under their dresses, open, exposing the pink nub just waiting for some attention.

When Zeke saw the woman in the gray dress, he noticed first her long neck, the upswept hair, the sad tilt to her head. Her eyes were dull and lacked fire; her gloves frayed and dirty. She held herself like a flower, but she was more of a weed. But when he held her hand in his own, he felt it. That peculiar fluttering that sometimes happened. A yearning within him. He could teach her a thing or two about love. About what being alive meant. He'd have taken her into a dark corner and shown her a thing or two right then, but there were so many eyes here. Not like in Chicago. In Chicago, a man could fuck when he wanted. Here, you'd have to do it in the dark, like an animal. He wanted no part of that.

Zeke was on a procuring mission. Auntie Mabel had sent him out to hire some new girls. Repopulate their garden with fresh flowers. He'd already snagged a dozen or more. A haul more bountiful than transporting Christmas trees, like he told people. And wouldn't Auntie Mabel be pleased with him for once.

With Cora's hand in his, he'd felt a stirring in his loins. An awareness that he could have her if he wanted. She wouldn't do for the house. Too old. Too sad. Too used up. But she'd do nicely for him. He imagined her pretty mouth wrapped around him, him pounding into her. Wouldn't that just shock the nice church people at the picnic here, to witness that.

But Zeke had work to do. He needed another twelve girls before he could go home. There were a few here, but no one as of yet, had responded to his promise of a theatrical life. The girls here were dull and sanded. No better than drift wood.

But when he saw the girl jumping in the sack, when he saw her pigtails bouncing and the blush in her cheeks, he knew. If he could snag that one, he could bring in a fortune.

And when he realized that the girl belonged to this woman, this Cora, it all locked into place.

Zeke took Cora's hand in his, and briefly dipped his thumb over under the fabric of her glove. He pressed. His body said: "I can teach you things". There was a sheen of sweat on her upper lip. Her pupils dilated. "You're the prettiest girl here, Mrs. or not," he'd said, and it was partly true. She was pretty. Women loved to hear that they were beautiful. It was the first step in owning them. He'd smiled, made his voice soft and supple. "If you do come, bring your girl, too. We have lots of jobs opening up."

He let go of her hand and smiled. The sun was warm and children laughed and the world was a good, good place.

❧❦❧❦❧

After the picnic and over the days that followed, Cora felt his thumb on her pulse point. It was a shock of electricity that allowed her soul to detach from her body and slip away. Soon, her soul would call to the rest of her, and Cora would follow. Really, in her spirit, she'd already left Michigan behind.

4

Papa said, "I'll be gone for a week, no more." They were eating a breakfast of sausage and potatoes, too heavy for the heat of early August, but it was all they had. Mother sat at the table, her plate pushed out in front of her. She'd gotten thinner lately, and there were deep shadows under her eyes.

"A week?" Lillian asked, both fearful and excited. A week without Papa, but a week on her own with Mother. Sometimes, it was as if her mother looked right through her, like Lillian was no more than a ghost. Maybe a week alone together would make her mother finally see her. Still, the house wasn't the same without Papa.

She felt like crying. She said, "I wanted to talk to you about the book!" The book he'd given her weeks ago, *Nature Biographies: The Lives of Some Everyday Butterflies; Moths; Grasshoppers and Flies*, was sitting next to her on the table. The pages were already dog-eared and worn with love. She'd read the first section over and over, explaining how butterflies metamorphosed from caterpillars into winged creatures. There were 150 photographs in the book. 150!

"And we will talk about it," Papa said gently. "In fact, why don't you work out some kind of presentation or experiment you can show me when I get back?"

Mother huffed. "Really, John. There's far more to do around here than have her read and work on fanciful *presentations*. What's the point of that?"

"The point, my sweet," he said as he pushed up from the table, his plate clean of every scrap, "is education. It would be nice if in the future Lillian could…"

"Find a good husband. That's all she needs to do. A *good* husband. One who provides fully." Mother turned her face away from them. Lillian had gone invisible, again. There was something vibrating between her parents, like a string pulled taut and plucked, but she wasn't quite sure what it was.

"Well, *this* husband is providing by going out onto the lake for a while. We'll bring in a huge catch, and I'll get a nice bonus for our orchard. For *our* future." He nodded his head to the biscuit tin sitting on the shelf. The tin that held not biscuits, but coins. One day, Lillian would add coins to it too.

"When you get back, Papa, I'll tell you all about the American Tent Caterpillar. It can eat a whole orchard in a week. Or something. I'll read up on it and let you know."

"You do that." He smoothed the front of his shirt. Sometimes his hands moved like they weren't a part of him. Like they belonged to someone else. "Well," he said, and Lillian knew that meant he needed to go.

She stood up and hugged him. He petted the top of her head. She liked the feel of his scratchy shirt against her cheek. "A week," he said. "Show me something then that you've learned."

With that, he grabbed his bag and headed out the door. Her parents did not say goodbye to each other. Lillian thought maybe because a week wasn't long enough to warrant a farewell.

A week turned into two, and her mother became all fluttery. There was a glow and heat to her cheeks as she raced around the house when Lillian came home from playing in the orchard, a glass jar filled with grass and a butterfly (or maybe it was a moth) she was going to pin to a board and present to her father when he returned. The color tickling Mother's cheeks was not a happy blush, but the red streak of a fever. She was wearing her best blue dress, the one she only put on for special occasions, and Lillian was confused. There was nothing special about today, but the dress said otherwise.

"Come!" she said when Lillian walked in the door.

"Where are we going? Is Papa home?" Her heart skipped a little. He would be so proud of all the work she'd done.

"We must hurry!" Mother called. She grabbed a chair and stepped up on it, reaching for the biscuit tin on the shelf. Only instead of dropping in a handful of coins, she took the tin down and emptied it into a bag.

"What are you doing?" Lillian asked, her voice tight with fear. Something was not right here. Not her mother's blush, her lightning movements, not taking their Cherry Orchard money from the shelf.

"We have to leave. Now." She turned to her, and Lillian gasped. Her mother seemed almost like someone else. There was a blackness swirling in her eyes. "Change your dress. We aren't taking anything. We need to leave, now."

Lillian felt the tears coming, like a giant wave crashing over her. "Where? Why? Where's Papa?"

"Papa isn't coming home. There was a storm. The ship was lost in Lake Michigan. And we need to leave *now*. Your father has left us with nothing, except for a big bill to the Millikens. Move. *Now!*" The words snapped out like a whip.

Lillian couldn't breathe. She slipped out of her body and watched herself run to her bedroom. She tore off her dress and grabbed the only other one she had available. The one she'd wear to church. Papa wasn't coming home? Papa's ship went down? It didn't make sense. He promised. He promised he would be gone for a just a week. Her mother called to her to hurry. Before she left, she grabbed the book her father had given her. Surely she could bring that if she could carry it.

"Let's go!" her mother cried. She grabbed Lillian's hand and they began to run.

Lillian looked back. The jar filled with grass and bugs sat on the table. The butterfly inside flapped its wings uselessly against the lid. There was no way for it to escape.

❧5❧

Cora had it all planned out. It hadn't taken any effort, really. It unrolled like a rug…one push and it unfurled all on its own. They would escape. She would protect Lillian, the way that she had dreamed of being protected, and she would whisk her away to a safe place. A place where Lillian could grow up and meet a good man who could support her the way she deserved, maybe buying a nice home for Cora too, though Cora wasn't quite past the courting stage, yet. If she weren't married. It didn't matter. This was a moment for a new start. To start the way life should: with possibility.

She took their cherry farm money. All of it. Cora moved with the speed of a crack of lightning. This was her chance, and she intended to take it.

John's ship had been delayed. He was not dead, of course. Not at the bottom of Lake Michigan, where, secretly, she thought he'd be better off. Happier. He was circling the Upper Peninsula where the fishing was better than expected. By the time he made it home, they'd have been gone long enough for a thin layer of dust to settle over every surface in the house, though he probably wouldn't even notice.

It was amazing how swiftly one could free oneself. Like throwing open the door to a cage, Cora had escaped, bringing her little bird with her.

They took a train to Ludington, and then boarded the ferry for Chicago.

On the train, Cora sat demurely. She folded her gloved hands in her lap and imagined she was a debutante at a ball. She should have been a debutante. She should have been swathed in white silk and passed from one fine-gloved hand to another. Instead, she was a fisherman's wife with calluses on her knees. That could stop now. The train shook on the tracks, and Cora felt as if it was shaking off her skin, leaving her exposed and soft as a peeled hardboiled egg. For once, Lillian did not prattle on and on. Her daughter sat in a stunned sort of silence, her eyes hollow. Her shoulders seemed weighted down. She'd get over it soon. Every girl had to leave her father, at some point. Every girl was handed over to someone new and forgotten. That was the way the world worked.

The train hummed, or maybe a song hummed within Cora's chest. The landscape rushed by in a zoom of color. She closed her eyes to it. When she opened them again, it would be like awakening from a bad dream, and she could start the day over again. Chicago was just a boat ride away. It waited for her.

❧❧❧❧

Lillian stood on the ferry's deck, squinting into the heavy wind. She couldn't see Chicago, yet, but the captain had announced they'd be able to see it soon. All Lillian could see was a strip of dark grey in the distance.

A gust of hot air slithered over her and was so fetid she could taste it. Was that Chicago? Did it have an odor? She wanted to ask her mother what it was from, that smell, but she wasn't sure where Mother was. Probably sitting below deck, trying to settle her stomach. Mother didn't like the water. If she caught a hint of the stench, she'd surely lose her lunch. Lillian, so like her mother, felt her stomach roil. She tucked her nose into the collar of her dress. She'd get used to the smell. She'd have to. Chicago was going to be their home now, and it seemed to wear a stench like a sweater. It wasn't at all the way she'd imagined it. What had she thought? The wind would smell of cotton candy, and the streets would be paved with gold?

Her father was dead and rotting at the bottom of the lake.

There was no gold left in her world.

It was fitting that Chicago stank.

It was a choppy crossing on Lake Michigan. In the middle of the lake, there was a good hour or two when Lillian couldn't see land at all. She tried not to think of all the stories she'd heard about the lake swallowing ships whole. She tried not to think about passing over decaying boats with men trapped on board, their bodies eventually mummified in algae. She tried not to think about Papa. When she thought about Papa, she couldn't breathe, and she needed to breathe to go on.

Mother was breathing just fine, when she wasn't feeling seasick. In fact, just looking at her, you wouldn't know that there was anything wrong at all. When they boarded the train, she sat so still with her hands clasped in her lap that she might have been praying. Lillian knew, though, that Mother didn't pray. What Mother was doing was planning. Her mother sat there in her good blue dress that was now stained at the edges, her white gloves now grey at the fingertips. The flaws in her mother's appearance seemed to sprout like mold on bread.

"What are we…" Lillian had begun, trying to ask her mother what they were going to do. Why did they run so fast? What happened to Papa, exactly? Why was everything different? But her mother had just given her a slight shake of the head, her hands clasped in her lap so primly, that Lillian knew it was best to be quiet. Her mother wasn't even in her own body.

Lillian lifted her nose away from her collar. Maybe the winds were shifting. Or maybe she was getting used to the smell. The waves around her sent a fine, cooling mist into the air. Lillian imagined this is what spiders felt like when they were spinning a web, covered in a fine warm mist.

There it was. Chicago stretched out before her. It reminded her of a carcass. The line of grey in the distance (closer now) had suddenly developed spines. She'd seen enough carcasses in the woods to know. Deer that hadn't made it through the starvation of winter. Their bodies left to rot in the woods and finally become part of the earth. Chicago looked like a deer on its side, left to rot long enough that it had lost the flesh around the broken rib cage, but not the flesh around the stomach. From this distance, she could see little shapes bustling about, white shapes wriggling like maggots. Carriages and horses, probably. People. Mother said there were more people walking Chicago's wharf than Lillian had seen in the whole of her life.

Lillian didn't care to see that many people. What was the point of that?

There were ships in the harbor. She could make out details, now. The foghorn burst out a call so loud that it shook Lillian's heart. She covered her ears, but the sound had already seeped into her, like everything else had seeped into her on this journey.

She could no more stop the ferry from anchoring at Chicago, than she could stop a train on its tracks once it had started moving. Not even if she lay down in front of it.

With each passing minute, with each rise and fall on the stormy lake, they were one breath closer to their new lives.

Lillian wished she could open her eyes and wake up from this. She closed her eyes tight, as tight as she could, thinking that if she could make her face hurt and force herself awake, that all of this would be a dream.

That was a childish thought and she tried to put it aside. Those kinds of thoughts were better left in Michigan, along with every other part of her that mattered.

She opened her eyes and watched without moving or thinking or breathing while the ship slowly pulled into port.

When the ferry docked, and the passengers disembarked, Lillian found her mother standing on the wooden planks just off the ferry. She slipped her hand into her mother's. They just stood there. Waiting. Lillian waited for her mother to pull her hand, to tug her, showing which way to go. But maybe Mother didn't know. Maybe she didn't have a plan, at all.

෫෧෫෧෫෧

Chicago was a different city, but it might as well have been a different planet entirely for how little it resembled the world Cora had always lived in. She couldn't move. She just stood there, breathing, dimly aware of the pressure of Lillian's hand in hers. She was waiting, but she didn't know for what.

She felt as if she were part of a giant beast, like she existed in its belly. There was the clacking and rumble of a cable car shrieking as it raced past. The sound of horse hooves thumping. The creak and shiver of carriages jostling on the busy dirt road. There were also voices—so many voices surrounding her that she almost felt as if they were coming from within her. Behind Cora and her daughter, the men on the ships barked orders at each other. The sails whipped in the breeze. A bell clanged. On the corner a newsboy stood on a broken crate calling out to buy the paper. "Hundreds perish in slaughterhouse fire!" he cried, and it sent a terrible thrill through Cora. Women's voices trickled in, too. "Flowers for a penny!" they cried. "Pretzels!" "Chinese fan to help with the heat, miss?" Women with wide hips pushed prams and cooed to babies. Children buzzed around their mothers and nannies in frantic circles. A boy wearing expensive clothes, shorts and a silk shirt, chased a girl in a flowered pinafore, her braids flapping against her back. They dodged legs and carts and horses, and wove around a man digging through the garbage, a man so thin that Cora could see the outline of his skeleton. She thought she should turn away, but his suffering pulled at her. The children circled him twice, and then ran back, past Cora and Lillian to whoever their keepers were.

There was motion and noise everywhere, so much so, that it became a sort of hum, as if Chicago (the beast) had ancient vocal chords and was trying to speak. The hum started to form into words, and Cora was certain a revelation was coming, something about her and hope and the future and love and money, something about a life so rich it seemed dipped in honey, but then she realized the words were only coming from Lillian. Lillian was calling her name. "Mother," she said, again and again, like she was whispering a curse.

"What?" Cora asked, irritation clinging to the word like sweat. She hadn't understood anything Lillian had said to her. On the best of days, with no distractions, it was hard to understand what Lillian jabbered on about. Bugs mostly. Life cycles. Ridiculous things. Today, understanding her was like trying to figure out a new language.

"Mother? Where do we go now?" It seemed as if Lillian emphasized every word so that each one burrowed into her skin. Cora looked at Lillian. She had cow eyes, big and brown and vulnerable. Cora wished she'd left her in Michigan but Ezekiel...

The thought of Ezekiel brought a blush to her already warm cheeks. Ezekiel had said she should bring Lillian, and so she had. And shouldn't she? She was Lillian's mother. She was a good person, and a good mother did not abandon her daughter, like her mother had done to her. Cora was better than that.

Cora reached into her frayed purse. Already she could see that her purse was hopelessly old-fashioned. She would buy a new outfit (head to toe) as soon as they were settled.

She pulled the card from her purse, though she'd memorized it as soon as he'd given it to her. She ran her finger across the words with her finger and it was as if she was tracing the curve of his lips. "We're going to The Garden Room. It says it's on Franklin Avenue." It sounded so sophisticated. Maybe she would have to get that new dress before she found him.

Cora smiled. She couldn't stop herself, and really, there was no need to hide, anymore. Here, she could breathe. She could move any way she wanted. What she'd been waiting for had finally arrived. She hadn't realized it, but her body knew. She'd just been waiting for her heartbeat to fall in sync with the rhythm around her. Now it had.

She pulled Lillian away from the ships and toward the line of carriages waiting to be hired and whisk them away. Cora felt alive, maybe for the first time ever. "Let's go," she cried, and it was a cry of joy.

❧❧❧

Mother pulled hard on her hand, and they ran, ran through the milling crowd; ran like they were both children. If Lillian's heart weren't broken, she might have laughed at the energy of their sprint, the sheer buoyancy of it. Instead of laughing, she just held on. Breathless, they arrived at a cross street. A trolley shook past, stuffed with people, its bells clanging. Her mother waved frantically, and an old man veered his horses to pick them up. His face was leathered. His body hard. "We've just arrived," Mother said to the man, as if he cared. "Isn't that wonderful?"

"*Wunderbar*," the man replied. "Where you go?" he asked, his accent thick and guttural.

"To the…" her mother paused. "I was going to say straight to the theater, but I think we ought to get out of these clothes. Do you know of a nice hotel? Not the nicest, perhaps. I'm a widow and…well…you know…a hotel that is comfortable?"

"*Ja*." The man said. He nodded his big head and flicked the reins and the horses clomped off, jerking them forward.

It seemed to Lillian that the world had sped up in its rotation. Things were moving too fast. There were too many people. Too much color. Too much noise and too many smells. She smelled rotting meat and flowers. Coal burning in the distance. She smelled the fishiness of Lake Michigan. Horse dung in the sun. Sweet grass threaded underneath. She felt covered in a thin sheen of sweat as if her whole body was crying. She wanted, more than anything, the soft sweet quiet of their little home near the orchard where she could run to the cherry trees, the fruit now heavy and ripe and sweet. She wanted Papa.

The ride seemed to take forever. Mother ooh'ed and ahh'ed at everything around them. The buildings tall as giants reaching for the end of the sky. The line of carriages congesting the road. People walking and carrying packages and umbrellas to ward off the gaze of the sun. The carriage jostled and rocked. Instead of soothing her, it made Lillian nauseous. Just as she thought she'd be sick, the carriage halted to a stop in front of a small building with a sagging front porch.

"Good rooms," the old man said, and with his thick accent the word 'good' sounded more like 'goot'. "German home. Good food."

German, Lillian thought. So he was German.

Mother paid him, her brows knitting when she heard the cost. Lillian noticed that her mother's purse looked lighter and she worried what this might mean.

Then she was whisked up the porch where her mother knocked on the door briskly. Her mother seemed so strong and sure of herself, as if crossing the lake had given her some kind of supernatural power. A child, four or five, opened the door. He was wearing a stained shirt and pants cut into shorts. His eyes were big and blinked slowly. He didn't say anything but ran off. A moment later, a round woman wearing a grey dress and a white apron came to the door. The dress was off her shoulder, the apron hanging loosely. She had a baby suckling at her fleshy breast, the white mound pillowy and lined with a deep blue vein, and Lillian turned away.

"I beg your pardon," Mother said.

"You want a room? Come this way. This way. Good room. Good food," the woman said, in that same German accent, ushering them in.

And quicker than she could understand, Lillian followed her mother up the stairs and into a small room with a thin bed pushed against the wall. The walls were covered with a wallpaper of pink roses. Everywhere, roses, but fake roses, one bleeding into the next. Roses so pink they seemed like their petals were made of tongues and they were screaming.

"We're here!" her mother said, her words musical.

Lillian sank onto the bed. It was done. They were here. There was nothing she could do about it, now.

⛧⛧⛧

Cora couldn't stop, not for a minute. She positively thrummed with happiness. Lillian lay on the bed, as useless as a pile of rags. Cora couldn't bear to look at her. Her child was like a weight wrapped around her middle, pulling her back to earth. Cora wanted to fly, but she couldn't fly with the current feathers she wore, stained and dull and so backwoods country. She'd once thought the blue dress she wore pretty, but now it's satin flowers at her waist were crushed and wilted. The hem of her dress heavy with dung-laced-dirt from the roads. She wanted something new. Something that would make her appear to the world as she felt; not like an old married woman, but a young girl, still filled with hope.

"I need to go out," she said, pulling off her dirty gloves and tossing them on the bed next to Lillian. "I need a new dress."

Lillian grunted, as if the child were becoming a beast. "You stay here and rest up," she continued. Her heart fluttered. Each word held her back. She wanted to run, to escape, to flee. "I'll come back later. With food or something and then…" She paused, thinking for a brief moment of the utter freedom of not coming back at all. She should feel sorry about that, guilty, she knew, but she didn't. So much of her life had been forced on her. A woman of no means had no choices, and Cora was tired of it. She couldn't abandon Lillian, though. Like it or not, there was something that tied them together, a cord much harder to sever than whatever had cleaved her to John. What would she tell Ezekiel when she found him? Out loud she said, "I'll come back soon. And then we can figure out what to do."

Lillian said nothing. She was already fast asleep. Cora turned and fled, out the room, down the stairs, out the front door and onto the bustling street. Outside she could breathe, again. She could feel her breasts pressing against the tight fabric of her dress. She wanted to be free of all of it. She was free. Finally!

She turned in a circle, taking in everything around her, the line of brick houses crammed so close together that they might as well have been one, giant long house, stacked with different colored bricks. She took in the horses tied up to hitching posts, their tails flicking against flies in the heat. The carriages strolling past, filled with men in business clothes and women who looked weary. These women, these kept Gibson Girls who were transformed into wives with their upswept hair and dresses trimmed with lace and feathers, did not know true weariness. They had maids and cooks, and their husbands kept lovers. All they had to do was have babies and look beautiful. The rest of the time they could eat cakes and fruit.

A woman with bright green eyes, sitting in the cab of a jostling carriage, held Cora's stare for a moment as she passed. She looked the same age as Cora, but her clothes were a deep green silk and she wore a feathered hat. Cora's appearance was a mark of shame. It was like walking around with a birthmark covering half her face. If only she could switch places with the woman in the carriage. If only she had a different kind of life. So much of a woman's happiness depended on what type of a cage she was kept in. Cora's cage was so old and rusted that the door had fallen off.

The woman passed and disappeared amongst the sea of travelers. Cora kept walking, determined. There was trash on the walkway. Light brown dirt puffed up and covered her shoes with a thin dust, making them look burnt. Still, the dirt and trash here was better than the dirt and trash in Michigan. At least, here it meant something was happening.

Cora realized she had no idea where she was, and no idea where to go. It should have terrified here. Instead, it made her laugh. She stood there, in her stained dowdy blue dress, the sun hot on her shoulders, the world whirling around her, and laughed.

❧ 6 ❧

All Cora needed to do was ask, she discovered. *"Where is the nearest dressmaker?" "Where do I find lunch?" "What street am I on?" "How do I get back to this boarding house?"* Strangers answered her and led her onward as if she was in a dance and they passed her hand to hand. She twirled and sashayed and spun, her feet hardly touching the ground at all. When she found herself in a dress shop on Michigan Avenue, breathing in the crisp clean scent of linen and new fabric, she felt like she'd walked into heaven. What she wanted most desperately was one of those Luna Moth dresses, made of diaphanous material and trimmed with lace and feathers. But she needed something she could wear in the day. The evening dress would have to come later, when someone, preferably Ezekiel, would buy it for her.

There was a bell that announced her arrival when she entered the shop. It was like walking into a carnival of clothes, the colors, the fabrics, everything bright and cheerful. Though the shop was small, every inch seemed to be swathed in color. Instead of a bookcase loaded with books like in a stuffy library, fabric in bright blue, green, red, orange, and pink sat stacked on the walls and reached the ceiling.

Dresses hung on racks, so close to each other that when Cora walked, she had to part the dresses with her fingertips to move forward, as if parting some enchanted curtain into a fairy land. These were dresses just waiting to be worn. Like some wonderful gift you need only point to and it was yours. Cora had made her own dresses, and spent hours and hours trying to get the seams straight.

The room swished with her movement, the sound of tiny waves cresting. There, a dress with tiny rosebuds embroidered on a pale mint sheath. Here, one with silver stripes woven into a purple fabric so that the dress seemed to glow.

"Can I help you, miss?" The shopkeeper asked, appearing from the back room, carrying a dress so shiny it could have come from the sun. She was a young girl, not much older than Lillian, and had a thick Irish lilt to her voice. Cora was discovering the truth that Chicago was crawling with immigrants.

"I need a dress," she said proudly, staring the girl in the eye. The girl looked her up and down, no doubt judging the sack she wore, with a look that questioned her ability to pay. Cora held the coin purse out in front of her. She'd spend it all if she needed to, just to prove she could. When she found Ezekiel, he'd give her that job in the theater and she'd have more money than she could count. Perhaps he'd even fall in love with her and they would be married by next summer. They'd have a wedding by the lake. "I want something bright," she said. "Something like a peacock might wear."

"Of course, miss," The shopkeeper said and curtsied. She abandoned the dress she was carrying to tend to Cora. "I think I have some things that would look just lovely on you. Bring out that natural color in your cheeks."

That was better, she thought. That was how she would be treated—as if she mattered.

❧❧❧

When Lillian awoke, the room was growing dark. New night sounds called just outside the window. Down below, she could hear the sharp words of German. The landlady, maybe, and her husband. The scent of cooking cabbage and sausage filtered in under the door and Lillian's stomach growled. Mother was going to bring back food, but Mother wasn't here, yet.

Maybe she wasn't coming back. Maybe she had joined Papa at the bottom of Lake Michigan. Lillian shook her head, trying to shake away the image of Mother in Papa's arms, him spinning her around and around on the sandy bottom of the lake while her hair floated around them, wrapping them in a web.

She scooted to the corner of the bed, the wall hugging her. With something solid behind her, she could remember where she was and what she was doing here. Papa was dead. Mother was getting a new dress so that they could start over. They were in Chicago, and the world and life was a good place. A place where good things could happen. Maybe if she repeated it enough, she'd believe it.

Lillian grabbed the book Papa had given her. It was the only things she'd had time to take, and she'd carried it on the train and then the boat, sometimes holding it like a shield. She opened the book and though the light was greying, she could still see the photographs clearly. Here, a chrysalis. The caterpillar somehow transformed as if by magic, breaking apart its tender skin to emerge as something new entirely. That's how Lillian saw it, but the writer of *Nature Biographies*, Clarence Moores Weed, was more technical:

> In this molting process the skin upon the head splits apart along the middle line of the upper surface...the caterpillar manages to withdraw its head from the old covering, and then to escape entirely, leaving the cast skin at one side.

Lillian closed the book. At home, under the cherry trees, she'd read this passage, and it had seemed fascinating, how a caterpillar could cocoon itself and entirely transform. Now, it was a horror. She could almost hear skin tearing and its exoskeleton snapping. She worried that her mother was cocooning, her bones fracturing and reforming. Soon her mother's skin would split apart and she would step gently out of it, dripping blood and muscle, and leave her former self behind.

Outside, she heard a woman calling "Come inside, Jack. It's Friday, and you can afford me on Friday!"

"What about on Monday?" a man slurred in response.

"I'll have taken all your money by then!" she called back and there was raucous laughter.

Lillian tried to pull herself into a ball, rounding her body like a potato bug. But burrowing into herself changed nothing, and her stomach cried to be fed.

❧❧❧❧

When Cora left the store, she felt lighter, as if a heavy wind could carry her away if she just spread her arms. Her new dress was wrapped in brown paper, scented to smell like lavender, and tied with a purple ribbon. She couldn't wait to put it on. It would be like stepping into a new self, casting her old self behind. She'd thought leaving would be enough to reinvent herself, but she wanted to look different on the outside, as well.

She did not have enough money for a carriage to the boarding house, but it was no matter. Even the dark seemed more full of possibility in Chicago. It wasn't completely dark here, after all. They were starting to light the gaslights on the road. Soon, everything would be electric, she'd heard, and wouldn't that be a wonder.

Other things were lighter about Cora now, too. Her purse, for one, held only a few coins. She'd used it all. Everything they'd scrimped and saved over the years had purchased the train tickets, the ferry, a night's stay at the German's house, and her new dress.

She wasn't scared, exactly, but knew that they would have to find Ezekiel soon. Maybe even tonight. Cora was so awake and alive that she couldn't imagine sleeping. She'd get to her room, transform into her new self and then set out to find her new love. He'd be so surprised to see her. Unlike with how she felt about her husband, Cora looked forward to seeing Ezekiel. She still remembered the feel of his thumb rubbing against the pulse point of her wrist. The way he said her name. The shape of his jaw when he turned away from her.

She walked on, not feeling the fatigue of her journey so far, or that her feet were pinched in her boots. When a gentleman on the corner called out to her in some language she didn't understand, she simply held her chin high and smiled. A lady wouldn't deign to acknowledge that sort of drunken call, especially when it wasn't in English.

It seemed to take no time at all until she stood before the boarding house. It was really a sad little place, and Cora deserved so much better. She'd never, with the exception of this new dress, been granted any of the things she deserved. That would all change.

She opened the door and walked in, giving a small nod to the poor German mother behind the front desk. Cora was grateful that she wasn't able to have more children. Lillian had been more than enough. Lillian had been such an even that Cora had nearly bled to death. She shouldn't be grateful that Lillian had taken away her ability to carry another baby to term, but she was. Children were a burden.

Her burden sat huddled in the bed, shivering, like she was caught in some snowstorm. "Light a lamp!" Cora called. "We are civilized people, after all," she said, her voice taking on an airy quality.

Lillian squinted at her. "Mother?" she said softly.

"Well, who else would I be? The Queen of England? I should be so lucky. Come on. Get up. We're going out."

"Out? But it's so late, and I'm hungry."

Cora felt the familiar prickle of irritation creeping along her skin. Nothing was ever easy for her with Lillian. Nothing. The girl was stubborn. "If you're hungry, then we need to go and get some food, don't we? Do you think the fairies are going to bring it to you?" Cora laughed, imagining it. "There are no fairies in Chicago," she said.

Lillian sat up, rubbed her eyes and then stood.

"You can help me on with my new dress. I'd throw this old thing out but maybe you'd like it when you fill out a little more." Cora was being gracious. Lillian had always loved this dress. The idea that she might one day fill it out made Cora a little uncomfortable, though she wasn't sure why.

"Can we come back after we've eaten? I'm very tired," the girl said.

Cora had so many plans. So many things she wanted to do, but there was this constant pull on her. She thought once they'd arrived at Chicago she would be fully free, but there was no true freedom to you when you had a child. Not until they married someone and became their husband's burden. "Yes, fine," she said, agreeing just to get the girl moving. Ezekiel was so close she could almost feel him breathing. "Let's go! Come on! The night is young! Help me on with the dress!"

❧❧❧

Lillian's feet were bricks as her mother tugged on her to follow. They ran downs the stairs and out the door. The landlady called to them "No running! No here!" and Mother laughed like a girl.

"Mother! Please!" she cried. "I'm so hungry! There's food inside. She's serving cabbage and sausage and potatoes. You can smell it even out here!"

Mother, in her new, too-green dress, painted and fish scale shimmery in the moonlight, let go of her hand, suddenly bereft of all energy. "You always do this," she said softly, but with an intensity that frightened Lillian. "You're such an infant. You ruin everything. Fine. We'll go back inside and you can have your *sausages*."

Her words were acid. "It's all right. I'm sorry," Lillian said, trying to make her words a salve. "I'm not really that hungry. I'm sorry I asked. We can go. I just need to wake up a bit more."

Mother rolled her eyes. "Wait here," she said and then she was gone, disappearing back into the boarding house.

Chicago was pushing away the dark with the glare of flickering gaslight. It was all too much. The wide dirt road with piles of horse dung. The houses lined up in a row one on top of the other. How the houses weren't built well and so they sort of leaned. The garbage and the heat and the dirt. Lillian closed her eyes. Everything was too bright and too loud and there was too much heat and too many sounds. She wanted wide green space and a house surrounded by birches and oak, and a rolling orchard with apple and cherry blossoms just awakening. Closing her eyes did not fool her senses.

She could not escape the stench, breathing into her face. It smelled sour. Like someone breathing on her. Lillian felt the man standing over her before she even opened her eyes. She was afraid to open them, but she forced herself too. "How much?" he asked her.

"Pardon?" she asked, trying to lean away from him. Looking up she could see the scruff of his beard flecked with gray. There was a scar on his chin where no hair grew. He leaned down and sniffed her neck and Lillian started to cry. "You're a pretty little thing, aren't you? How much for a…"

And then Mother was back and shooed the man away. "Beast!" she cried. "You beast!" Lillian clung to her mother, who had, at last, done something to protect her.

The man stepped backwards, swaying a bit. "If you change your mind…" he said. "I'd pay a dollar for that."

Lillian wasn't sure he'd give her mother a dollar for, but she knew it had something to do with her.

"Go. Away." Mother breathed.

When he was at last gone and disappeared beyond the haze of light, Cora wriggled out of Lillian's grasp. "Here," she said and thrust a roll and a chunk of cheese into Lillian's hands. "You can eat while we walk."

Lillian didn't feel like eating anymore. She felt like being sick, but she bit into the hard roll, dotted with skinny seeds, and chewed. It was like chewing bark.

She didn't want to ask but she couldn't stop herself. "Where are we going?"

It was so dark now that the sky was dotted with stars.

"We're going to find Ezekiel," her mother said.

Lillian did not know who that was, but the way her mother said it, he sounded important. Maybe he was someone who knew father. Maybe he could help them go back home.

The houses they walked past ceased to look like separate identities, and instead became a segmented insect, like a millipede. One brick house linked to another, over and over and over, people crawling about like tiny legs.

She surrendered to her mother's force and just let her sweep her onward, as if she were a dinghy in a rough storm pushed by the angry waves.

Each heavy footstep forward sank Lillian further into her mind. Papa is at the bottom of the lake she thought. Papa has no eyes. Fish swim in and out of his skull. Papa is gone forever. I never got to say goodbye.

Mother was talking, but Lillian couldn't hear her, not anymore. We could be at home and maybe the Millikens would forgive the money we owe. We could have a burial for Papa, and I could visit him under the cherry trees, or plant an apple tree for him. Pastor Tom could say a eulogy and I could ignore him and listen to the wind in the trees, and in the spring I could look for morel mushrooms and wild leeks like Papa showed me, and I would cook them and eat them and remember all the things he ever taught me. I could grow up there and heal, and Mother would love me.

But Chicago was a different world, and her mother, encased in a dress of mossy green with orange accents, looked like a rotting peach. Mother was not Mother anymore. Mother was a beast. And Papa was dead. And Lillian could no longer be a child if she was going to survive. She would need to build a chrysalis around herself. And so she started with her thoughts.

My father is dead. My mother is a beast. And I am strong and able to fight this.

They ran. Lillian no longer cared in what direction.

∂7∞

There was something about the sound of the oncoming train that lulled Cora into memory, pushed her back, back, back in her mind. She'd been eight years old when her mother had died in childbirth. Cora had huddled in her bed, clutching Dolly to her chest. When the midwife came out of her mother's room, Cora already knew. Not because of the bright blood on the midwife's apron, but because there was no more screaming. Her father took Dolly out of her arms and replaced it with a wriggling newborn. Her brother. A real live baby doll. She never held Dolly again. Her father tossed her into the fire along with her mother's bloodstained clothes and blankets.

By nine, she had taken over her mother's wifely duties. She cooked, she raised her brother, and at night, her father sometimes crawled into her bed, smothering her with affection. In the morning, he warned: "If you ever say a word of this…" He did not need to voice the words. Cora knew that if she spoke, she would die, too, and so she became silent.

She met John when she was fifteen. He was twenty. She was shopping at the market, and he had just come onshore with a load of fresh whitefish, the fish gasping their last breaths. "I'll take that one," she said softly. She pointed to the smallest. "Oh, now, that one's no good. Why not take this one? It's the same price," he said. But she knew that wasn't true. He smiled at her, then.

He was tall and young and good, and he looked at her like she was good, too. When he started courting her, she felt like she was finally given the key to her prison. "Cora, you're the most beautiful girl I have ever seen," he said breathily. "I have got plans," he said. "I can't offer you much now, but one day I am going to stop fishing. I am going to buy a whole orchard full of cherry trees. We'll be rich. And I will buy you those fancy dresses like the Millikens are always wearing. You should be wearing clothes like that."

She'd blushed. It was like John was giving voice to her innermost secret desires, shaping them into song. "Marry me," he said, holding out his hand in promise. She nodded because she believed him.

Her father grudgingly gave his approval. It was luck that Cora wasn't carrying his child, and maybe he knew that luck had a way of running out. Insisted he would marry the next-door neighbor's girl. She would be pregnant immediately.

At sixteen, Cora married John. John crawled on top of her at night and Cora knew that his promises weren't ever going to come true. John was a liar, just like her father, and his constant need to smother her was proof of it. Cora was pregnant within weeks, and there were no cherry trees or orchard, and she wore a brown dress so stiff and scratchy that it left marks on her smooth skin. The truth was that women were cattle, to be mounted and then to give birth. For years, Cora endured this until suddenly...

She'd run and run and run, and now, for the first time, she was running toward something and not away. Maybe Ezekiel would turn out to be like all the other men she knew, but there was one small difference. Cora wanted him. She wanted his young firm hands on her breasts. She wanted to devour him. It was the first time she'd ever felt desire for something physical. It was a drug, and she wanted more.

In her mind, Ezekiel offered all the things denied to her: pleasure, security, fame, hope.

She ran, tugging Lillian along with her. They were so close. So very close now.

❧❧❧

Lillian wasn't sure where they were exactly, but she knew it wasn't a good place. Good places did not shift and creak like the planks beneath their feet. Good places did not whistle and moan like the boats docking behind them. Good places did not hiss and scream like the trains and automobiles and carriages. Good places were quiet. Good places lapped and hummed and sighed.

This was not a place where good people went. This was a place made for the shadows. This was a place where nightmares breathed.

Mother grabbed her hand, and they ran and ran and ran. As they slowed to a stop, both of them breathing hard, Lillian's feet on fire with the pain of movement, she saw a woman standing in a doorway, her long hair unpinned flowing over her bare shoulders. She was naked. She stood in the doorway her chin tilted up as she smoked on a cigarette. Lillian didn't want to look, but she couldn't stop herself. The woman had large breasts, pendulous almost, with nipples that were brown and the size of Lillian's fist. There was hair between her legs reaching almost to her belly button. She had wide hips and a scar on her shin.

The woman said something to her and started to laugh. Lillian turned away. Her face now as hot as her feet.

"Here we are," Mother cried in that happy way she had that didn't feel quite real to Lillian. Mother's voice was like a like a delicate piece of glass that if held too tightly would shatter in your hands. "The Garden Room!"

It was not a theater. There was music spilling from the house, but this was no theater, even Lillian knew that. A theater had a marquee and stage bills and a ticket booth. This had a big man standing at the front, and though there were lights, every window illuminated from within, the shadows showed the figures of men and woman together. Their bodies fusing the way that dragonflies fused when mating, becoming a single creature, monstrous and obscene. Lillian wanted to hide behind Mother, crawl under her dress like when she was little and pretend no one could see her.

Papa is at the bottom of the lake, she thought, and a few spindly threads wrapped around her heart, protecting her.

Mother walked right up to the man. He was so big that Mother had to look up to talk to him. He was completely bald, and his head shone in the gaslight. His nose was flat and lay too far to one side. He had a voice that was deep and broken, as if his vocal chords had either not formed at all, or someone had crushed them. "What you want little woman?" he asked. He licked his lips as if tasting something sweet.

"Ezekiel Thatcher," Mother said softly, and then with more force, "I'm here to see Ezekiel. He's expecting me. Us. He's expecting us."

"Is he now? Expecting you?" the man asked, and then a rumble formed in his chest. Lillian guessed it was his way of laughing. "Ezekiel is detained," he said, emphasizing that last word to make it mean more than just its definition, only Lillian couldn't figure out what more it could mean.

"Well, I never told him when we'd arrive, exactly, but I can assure you," Cora paused. Lillian wondered why. "He invited me here, and I'm here, now, and I'd like to see him. Please, sir."

"Awww, now, since you called me sir, go right on in. But leave the girl here. I've a feeling that what's inside there might be a little too harsh on her virgin eyes," he looked Mother up and down and licked his eyes, again, "But not, I expect, too harsh on yours, Madam."

He stepped aside, allowing Cora to pass. "Stay here, Lillian," she said without looking at her. "Go stand by the lamppost in the light. I'll be back in just a moment."

She watched her mother disappear into the bright house. Tinny music wormed its way under Lillian's skin and made her heart thud. A swarm of bugs buzzed by the gaslight's flame, wanting so much to be close to the gold center that they died trying to reach it. Lillian wrapped her arms around the post. She closed her eyes and began to count. She would just count and not think about Papa and the fish swimming through his cheeks. She would think of the green, green hills and the cherry orchard in bloom with petals unfurled, a white so delicate and beautiful that the petals blushed, embarrassed by their own beauty.

"Hold on tight," the big man on the porch called to her. "You might get hurt if you let go!" And then he laughed again, that laugh that felt like an assault. Lillian counted to one hundred, and then started over and counted again and again and again.

જાજાજા

Cora knew what this was, and this was no theater. It was a spectacle of sorts, the women half-dressed or naked falling over the men in suits as if they were human scarves. Three men sat in front of a fireplace, a woman on her knees in front of one, her head bobbing up and down. Cora caught glimpse of his maleness, consumed by a woman's mouth. Another man sat in a chair and a woman stood above him playing with his lips with her foot as if feeding him her toes. She wore only a thin robe in a gauzy material, exposing her very center to him. Cora closed her eyes, but then decided it was no good. She'd already seen too much.

"Are you here for work?" a female voice said. Her voice was older and edged with steel. Cora turned and saw a woman standing by the staircase. Her hair was cherry-red—bright, unnatural, and piled upon her head. She was so painted that Cora could see the cracks in her cheeks. Or maybe that was the wrinkles trying to show under the frosting. Her blue eyes were lined with coal and bright blue eyeshadow went clear to her eyebrows. There were two perfect red circles on her cheeks and her lips were stained a beet red. She was a big woman. An obese woman, and her purple silk dress seemed to strain itself to cover her rolls. "We're not currently looking for anyone…of your age," the woman said.

"Oh, of course not," Cora stammered. "I'm looking for Mister…Thatcher? Ezekiel? He's expecting me." Cora ignored the laughter coming from the front room, but it was hard to ignore the woman giggling as she pushed past them, her naked breasts swaying and a man chased her upstairs saying "I'm going to get you, I'll get you!"

"Ezekiel, huh? Expecting you?" The woman chuckled. "Let me show you to his office, and I'll see if he's finished his…work." When she paused, she motioned with her head upstairs and Cora knew what his work was. He was no different from other men, then. Just a brute looking to fill his needs with any empty vessel. "What's your name, honey?"

"Cora. Cora March. But he won't…I'm sure he won't remember my last name. Tell him…tell him I met him at a picnic. In Traverse City, Michigan. Tell him it's the woman with the jam."

"The jam, huh? That's a new one. The jam." The woman heaved herself up the stairs, chuckling, as if what Cora had said was funny.

Cora tried to breathe steadily. She focused on the piano music, how it thunked and twanged. The house was bustling with motion, like she'd stepped into a party. It wasn't so bad, really. At least, here, men were up front about their desires. Curiously, the women seemed to be enjoying themselves. In a back shadow, Cora noticed a younger woman pushing a man to his knees. "Kiss me," she heard, only he wasn't kissing her mouth.

She felt the blush through her entire body. What must that be like? To tell a man what you wanted? To actually feel pleasure for once. Cora wondered how much they were paid. As a wife, you had to give it away for free. At least, these women were compensated.

She turned her head and looked up the stairs. Even before she saw him, she sensed him. Her body reacted before her brain even registered his presence, and then there he was. Ezekiel. The first man she ever actually wanted to put his hands on her. He stood at the top of the stairs, looking down, searching, and then their gazes locked. His hair was disheveled, and he smoothed it back with his hands. "Well now," he said and he grinned. He was a charmer, all right, Cora thought.

She'd forgotten what he'd looked like. In his mind what she remembered wasn't really his appearance, but how she felt when he sat next to her on the bale of hay. His thumb tracing her pulse point. How his words were a feather on her skin. He was younger than she'd remembered. Not long out of boyhood, really. A man of twenty-three at most. She was twenty-nine. Almost thirty. She must seem so old to him.

He seemed to dance down the stairs. John had moved as if his feet were bricks but this boy, this man, tripped along, light and buoyant. Then he was standing in front of her. "What brings you to the Garden Room, ma'am?"

Ma'am, she thought. Ma'am? "Don't you…It's me. Cora," she said, her throat tight. "Cora March."

He looked at her blankly. "Are you collecting money or something?"

Cora was confused. "Pardon? Money?"

"Are you trying to save our souls? You're in the wrong place. The only thing we save around here is enough stamina for a second round." He laughed then. Cora could see he was missing a back tooth.

"I don't understand," she tried again. Maybe it had been too long. Maybe in her new dress she looked different than he remembered. "You invited me here. We met at the picnic in Michigan? You wanted...You wanted me to come and visit you here. And my daughter, of course. You invited both of us. You said you might have some work...in the theater?" Cora felt her hair standing on her arm and the back of her neck but not with desire. Someone was walking on her grave. This was the first tickle of fear.

He looked her over, his dark eyes searching. "Daughter, you say? How old is she?"

"She's eleven. Nearly twelve now. We...you and I...we had a *connection*." She whispered the last word, embarrassed that she had to remind him of what had been so evident to her.

"Ah. Eleven or twelve. It's beginning to come back to me. We might have space here for her. If she's a daisy, I'll give you a pretty penny for her. Then you could afford to get yourself some decent looking clothes."

Cora couldn't breathe. The room began to spin. Her dress, her beautiful new dress that she had paid so dearly for? Wasn't decent? Wasn't beautiful? Shame spread through her like a fever.

She had been so...misled. He didn't want her. He didn't even remember her. He wanted Lillian. For this house. This house that was not a theater or a garden, but a den of sin. Cora felt her stomach churning. She spun and ran for the door, for the street, anywhere to get out of this place that smelled of sweat and alcohol and sex, this place where naked men and women laughed at her in time with the clanging of a badly tuned piano, she had to get out, get away, fly fly fly.

She couldn't seem to get the door to open. The doorknob wouldn't turn. She couldn't see anything clearly. It was all blurring. She felt his hand on her arm. He burned her. "Hey, now," he said.

"Hey." She stilled. Froze. A trapped bird waiting for the clamp of its predator's jaws. "I remember you now. There was a pie contest."

She turned to him, but could not meet his gaze. She didn't know whether she should smack him or embrace him. "Yes," she said. It was all she could get out.

"What's your name, again?"

"Cora."

His grin was back. "There's something about you," he said. He gently touched her chin with his fingertips, lifting her face to look at him. "I remember I wanted to know if you taste like cherries. Do you?"

"I don't…"

He kissed her, and everything stopped. His lips were softer than John's. A boy's lips. But there was pressure there. And then there was pressure against her body, low down, where he reached a hand and cupped the most sacred part of her. She couldn't move. She didn't want to move. He broke the kiss and looked at her. His eyes were stormy.

The woman with the red hair broke the moment. "She might not taste like cherries there, but what about her other lips?" Then the woman laughed and laughed and laughed.

Zeke looked at Cora and seemed to ask her a question. Then he turned and walked out of the house. Cora waited for a moment, her blood coursing through her, trying to decide how to answer.

༺❦❦༻

Did Zeke remember her? Did he? He remembered the curve of her neck and the image of a flower spread wide open, it's stamen thick and glistening calling for a bee to rub against it. He would take her. Not take, exactly. He would…give himself to her. Show her what pleasure was. And then he'd take from her. A small price. Her daughter's hand maybe.

But later.

Right now, she was following him and that was enough. He liked being the one to lead.

༄♠༄♠༄♠

Cora was alive. She followed Zeke to the back of the house, let him lead her into the shadows, and when he kissed her, she felt the air fill her lungs and her sluggish blood begin to pump anew. She wanted. She *wanted*. This was new. This was never-before.

"Open up," he said to her, and he pressed her against the wall, and she knew what he meant. She lifted her skirts to him. She did! On her own. She lifted her skirts and he ripped at her underthings and he grabbed her leg and clasped it around him and he took himself in his hands, that beast, that thing she'd grown to hate, and he pushed it into her, but then, oh, then, with his hot hand, he pressed something below, something that was the very heart of her and Cora...she floated.

Oh, god. She breathed. This is what I have been searching for all this time, and I just didn't know.

༄♠༄♠༄♠

The bugs sizzled above her when they kissed the heart of the gaslight. Lillian still clung to the lamppost as if it was a ship's mast and she was holding on during a storm. Everything made her think of her father. It was enough to bend her knees and fall to the ground, so she just held on.

She heard a door slam and looked up to see her mother running, only she didn't run to Lillian, but down the porch and around the corner. She was being followed by a tall, thin man with a mop of brown hair. The bald man on the porch yelled "I bet I know which one of them is going to get a prize!" And laughed.

Lillian didn't know what to do. Where was her mother going? Why didn't she take her with her? Should she follow? Wait? What if that man did something bad to her? Then Lillian would be all alone in the world. She let go of the lamppost and stumbled after them, into the dark beyond the gaslights' reach.

Her mother was a flash of white, a flicker of candle and then she was gone. Snuffed out. Lillian tumbled forward, around the porch of the big house and into the alley, walking not by sight but by a sound as thin and tremulous as a blade of hair.

It seemed like she searched forever. She was in the alley and stumbled on something in the dirt. Shadows became menacing monsters, leering over her. "Mother," she tried to call out, but it came out more like a pinched whisper. Lillian was five years old again, having lost her mother in a crowd at the market, calling and calling for her. "Mother?" She tried again.

What she saw made her stop cold. Her mother was pinned against a the back of the house, her dress bunched around her waist, her legs wrapped around the tall, thin man with the mop of brown hair. He was heaving into her, fusing himself to her so that they became a giant dark beetle. And there were sounds too. Animal sounds. Grunting. A moan or whine coming from her mother. "Mother?" Lillian cried again.

The man stilled.

"Go away," Cora called to her in a voice that was not quite her voice. "Just go, Lillian." Her mother spat the words at her. She spat. "Now!"

Lillian backed up, turned and ran back to the only safety she'd felt since arriving in Chicago. To the long cold lamppost where she could stand still and hold on and hold on and hold on and on and on.

PART TWO

SUMMER

1910

TRAVERSE CITY, MICHIGAN

AND CHICAGO

8

JOHN 1899

I am marrying Cora today. There is a part of me that don't believe she said she'd take my hand. I am twenty-one years old to her sixteen and must seem old to her. She...she is everything I did not know I wanted and needed. To think of life without her, well, it wouldn't be worth getting up in the morning.

I am in my father's house, getting dressed, when he comes in. He has had two fits in the last three years and his left side don't work the same, anymore. He uses a cane, and his face is tighter than it used to be. I know he wants to have a talk with me, and I had hoped that we could avoid it, like we avoided most of the things that need to be said.

"John," he says, and I know what is coming. "Don't marry that girl." And God help me, I want to punch him. I cannot say a word for fear I might actually do it. I have never wanted to be violent with my father and this is a new and dark thing between us. "There's something in her eyes, son." He says, his words ugly and twisted.

"She's not the satisfied type. She's going to want more from you than you can give."

I could defend myself. I could say I can give her my love and in a few years time we will have an orchard and more money than we can count, but the old man is nearly deaf, whether because of the fits or because he just does not like to listen to me, I don't know. Or maybe he is just being critical because he is old and he is not man enough to love anymore. What he has said is enough. He has said his peace. Now he can shut up about it.

"Marry a plain girl," he says. "A plain girl you could make happy."

"Not now," I say and it is the first time I've said anything to cross my father, but I have a feeling it won't be the last. I look in the mirror. I see who I am, but I also see who I will be. I will wait for Cora by the willow tree and the creek and she will wear white and she will take my hand and we will be married. I will make her happy because my love for her is that wide. She looks at me like I have the power to change the world, and I mean to prove to her that I do.

I turn away from my father and walk out of the house, toward the preacher, toward Cora, and all the beauty that lies in front of us.

❧ 9 ❧

JUNE 1910

Cora checked her purse, again. How had this happened? One week in Chicago and their money was gone? All of their money? She tried to do the math in her head. The cost of the train tickets, the ferry, the four dollars for the room and board for the first week, the new dress, and then the nights out with Ezekiel. Well, Zeke, she called him, now. "Every time you use my full name, I feel like I'm being scolded," he'd said to her just last night while they lay in his bed at the Garden. "Call me Zeke," he kissed her then, the soft line in between her breasts, "unless you really are scolding me. Then call me whatever you like." Zeke liked her best when she was fighting him. Too many women offered it up, he said, but Cora was something special. "Zeke," she'd said. "Keep kissing."

Now, she stood in her room with Lillian whining again about being hungry. The next week's rent was due today and there was no way Cora could get four greenbacks in a day. "When we go down to eat," Cora advised Lillian, "Eat as much as you can. Fill up. And put some bread into your bag. After we eat, we need to pack up and head out."

"Where will we go?" Lillian asked, her voice hollow, to match her eyes.

Questions, questions. Lillian always asked questions, and it ground on Cora. "Never you mind. We just need to go." Cora would figure this out. Ezekiel, Zeke, might loan her some money, or know of a place she could get some work. She knew what kind of work he offered at the Garden Room, and she wasn't ready for that kind of earning. She enjoyed what he did to her body. For the first time in her life, she understood what pleasure from sex was, and she wasn't about to trade that pleasure in for a few lousy coins and another set of sweaty hands on her. Zeke's hands were soft as a boy's, but the rest of him…well, Cora smiled, the rest of him was hard.

"Why do we have to pack up, Mother? I like it here. Mrs. Schultz is nice and I could be all right with staying right here. There's a school not too far that some of the Schultz kids go to. I could…"

Cora didn't bother looking at her. "You need to get it through your head, Lillian. You're not a child anymore. There isn't time for school. You'll need to find some work to do and we need to find a new place to stay. One that's not quite as cushy. At least until we find someone to take care of us."

Of course, Ezekiel could take care of them. Ezekiel's income from the Garden Room would be enough to buy one of those nice brick houses by the shopping district. Cora would wear a feathered hat and a light green dress with lace during the day, and at night she'd have dresses in a rainbow of colors, one for every mood. But a week was not enough time to convince him. She'd need a month, maybe two. They would have to tighten their belts for two months. Lillian especially. The girl was old enough now to carry her own weight. Cora had been only eight when she'd been forced to grow up. Nine by the time her father treated her like his own. She refused to think about that now. She thought about moving forward. Moving on.

"Let's get breakfast, and then we need to get out. No more discussion, Lillian. No more questions. Do you hear me?"

But the girl didn't answer. Cora didn't look at her to see why.

❧❧❧

Lillian didn't know why she was crying, she just was. Something had happened, and suddenly all the tears she didn't cry in the last few weeks, welled up in her and stormed out. She tried not to make a sound, but since she couldn't seem to stop the tears, she just let them out. Her mother packed up the few things they had into their carpetbag, but Lillian still clutched her book. It was the last bit of Papa that she had to hold onto, and she wanted him close to her. Cora waited, looking out the window to the street below, until Lillian's tears finally dried up. "Thank you, Mother," she whispered and Mother gave her a curt nod in response.

When they went downstairs for breakfast, Lillian wasn't hungry, but she ate the sausage and cabbage anyway, to be good for her mother. Maybe if she was very, very good and stopped asking so many questions and being so difficult, maybe then Mother would see that it wasn't Lillian that made Chicago so miserable, it was just a miserable place on its own. When the wind hit just right, you could smell rotting meat in the air from the Slaughter district. People dumped piss pots into the streets. Garbage festered outside houses, and no one cleaned up after the horses. But her mother danced around like she was enchanted. Like she couldn't see the goblins in the market, the way that Lillian could.

The sausage in front of her was boiled and looked almost human-like. When she pierced it with her fork, the skin popped and split. Lillian cut a tiny piece and chewed it over and over until she could swallow it. She didn't want to leave here, unless they were leaving to go back home, but somehow she knew that wasn't possible anymore. Her mother was becoming someone else, and it was someone who wouldn't belong in Michigan.

"We'll find you something to do," Mother said, shaking Lillian from her thoughts.

"What's that?"

"For work, Lillian. Work. I'll have to get something, too. Maybe I can be a shop girl and work in one of those lovely clothing shops. Better than some Irish girl just off the boat. You could work in a factory or something. They make plenty of stuff here. Shoes. Clothes. Mattresses. Or maybe you could work on one of those farms."

"The slaughterhouse?" Lillian was terrified of this.

Cora laughed. "Well, it's not like they'd give you a butcher knife and say go to it. They have jobs for young women like yourself that don't involve slitting the animal's throats."

Lillian cut another piece of her sausage. She thought she saw it twitch.

"You'll need to make four or five dollars a week to pull your weight. I can't be the only one taking care of us. It's time for you to do your share. Your father coddled you way too long. It's time you…"

Lillian closed her eyes, squeezing them. Her mother mentioned Papa with ease, with no sense of longing or loss. He was just another discarded item to her mother, and it made Lillian angry. A few red threads wrapped around her heart. Red for anger. They wriggled in among the black threads for loss, and the blue for pain. Lillian didn't want to work. She wanted to go to school. She wanted to laugh and run and play and be a child. There didn't seem to be any choice. She hoped to find a job that would make her mother happy with her, at least.

"We'll start looking as soon as you finish." Then Mother lowered her voice. "I'll go up in a minute and get our bag. Wait until you see me leave until you join me. I'll wait for you outside."

Lillian knew then that her mother owed the German landlady money, and the landlady would not get it. She was a nice woman with five children and a husband who worked constantly to support them. Lillian would have to write a note in the back of her book so that she could, one day, repay the woman for what they owed.

"There," Mother said, wiping at her mouth with a napkin. She spoke quietly. "I'll go up. You wait a bit before you join me."

Lillian nodded and watched her mother go.

What if she didn't wait for her? What if mother just kept on going? It was the first time that Lillian realized how weak the threads were that tied them together. All her mother had to do was pull tightly, and that thread would snap, and Lillian might never find her, again.

❧·❧·❧

John March stood in the kitchen of his home not understanding. He'd stayed on the ship extra long to make a bonus and had a pocket filled with money. Enough money that, combined with their savings in the tin, they could buy a small plot of land and get started on their dream. Farmers in Traverse City were saying that cherries were a gold crop. The environment was perfect. Soon, they'd ship cherries all over the country. John could make a fortune, but he'd have to get in now. And now he could. But something was wrong.

The kitchen was quiet. His and Cora's room was quiet. Lillian's room was quiet. There were dishes on the kitchen table, grown hairy with mold. He'd been gone a total of three weeks, and he'd come back to a new world.

Did John know that she'd left him? Did he? There was no note. No sign of trouble before he left. But then…if he thought back…

An image of the picnic came to him. Of Cora, twirling and laughing. Of how she stopped when she saw him approaching. He knew the truth of it then; he probably knew it on his wedding day. His father, rest his soul, had been right all those years ago. Cora had the eyes of a woman who would never be satisfied.

John slumped down in a chair at the kitchen table, the green bills clutched in his fist. He already knew that the tin filled with their savings was empty. He knew too, that though their house was still filled with all the things they'd collected over the years, it might have been empty, because Cora had taken Lillian with her.

He might have let this moment break him, but he had work to do. He'd have to find out where they went and bring his daughter back. Cora…she could stay gone. The fishing line connecting them had snapped.

❧10❧

Their new home was not a home like what they'd had in Traverse City with her cozy room and the horses, and the orchard, and the bay. This was a room in a slanted brick boarding house, in the Packinghouse district. Lillian had thought the boarding house with the Schultzes was bad enough, but this was something else entirely.

The road was thinner here and marked with big holes. When it rained, the holes filled with water or horse piss. The houses weren't houses really, but a line of shacks, haphazardly nailed together. There were large brick buildings with thin hallways and built with as many rooms as the joists could bear. The walls were thin and marked with holes. On the street, people were thin, their eyes too big for their faces. This was a working class district, home to immigrants and the poor and the neglected.

And the place they stood before now, the slouching brick apartment building, had a feeling of sadness to it. If a house could give up, this one had long ago. "Don't you dare complain," Mother said. "It's your fault we're here. If you can get a job and get us some money, then we'll live in a better place. So you better find something, and quick."

They followed the sweaty landlord up three flights of creaking stairs. There were mouse droppings in the corner. The stairs were uneven. Lillian could hear other people in their rooms; babies crying, fighting couples, peculiar rhythmic thumping. The room rented for a nickel by the night. They did not have any money left but Mother said she made an arrangement with the owner, and he would give them the first three days free. By then, Mother said, Lillian would have a job and could start earning her keep. "It's a hole, daisy, but it's only temporary." Mother was starting to talk like someone else, now. Her words had changed along with her voice. She rouged her cheeks and lips too. Lillian wondered if she was going to sprout wings from her carapace. Not butterfly wings, of course, but beetle wings. Wings of a flying cockroach.

"Stop looking at my back," Mother said, annoyed. "I'll take the bed and you can sleep over there." She pointed to a corner across from her bed and near a scraped vanity, its mirror foggy. Lillian didn't say anything. "We'll get you something soft to lay down on. It's only temporary, for crying out loud, Lillian. The faster you get working, the faster we'll be out of here."

Lillian tried not to notice the walls but they were papered in what might have been cream-colored stripes at one time, but now had faded to yellow. The room smelled like smoke and sweat and something faintly of the lake. The swamp during mating season, Lillian decided. The room itself was swampy. There was a window, but the air was completely still and close. There was a single picture on the wall, a painting of a rose, and even that was faded. This was a sad room. A place where people came to give up. Lillian had to get out of here. "Can you help me find a job, Mother? I'm ready to help."

"Glad to hear it. That's the first sensible thing you've ever said. I'll ask Zeke. He knows all sorts of wonderful things. He even introduced me to the landlord here and helped out with the *arrangement*. He's a wonder, that Zeke. He knows more than your father ever did about…"

But Lillian didn't want to hear Mother talk about Papa. When Mother talked about him, he became a little more dead, and Lillian needed him living. "When is he coming?" Lillian asked. "Mr. Thatcher I mean?"

"Oh, six, I guess. He's taking me to the theater. So much culture here, isn't there? It's so wonderful, isn't it?"

Lillian wondered if her mother could actually see where they were living? Could she see the stained walls, the scarred floor? The water stained ceiling? Could she hear the cattle crying in fear before being slaughtered? Did she have any idea the life they were really living? Or was she still floating in some make believe debutante ball, the one where she was the star, and she never grew up? Lillian knew things about her mother, things she never spoke of. And the first was how she wasn't quite right in her mind. Not quite right, at all.

"It is wonderful," Lillian said. "Can I use a blanket from the bed?"

"For what? Are you cold? How is that even possible?" Her mother had forgotten already as she looked at herself in the foggy mirror and pinched her cheeks to bring out some color.

"For something to lay on. To soften the floor. Until we can get something else."

"Oh. Right. Of course. Take the top one. For now. When it gets cold, I'm sure I'll need it back."

When it gets cold. That phrase terrified Lillian more than anything else had. It meant that Mother intended that they stay. Maybe, just maybe, there would come a time when Lillian would leave her mother instead of the other way around.

She grabbed the blanket, heavy and damp from the heat, and moved it to the corner. She sat down and flipped open her book to the postcard that marked her place.

The cherry trees were in bloom. Lined up like aging ballerinas, their tender arms stretched and fluttering in the breeze. The flowers weren't white, but the palest pink imaginable; a blush really, trembling slightly, held up by gnarled brown fingers and cracked wood. The dancers stood as if holding a pose, waiting for the next note to carry them forward. Down the green hill they'd tiptoe, past the emerald oaks and maples, and into the cool blue of the bay that lay waiting, just beyond reach.

The postcard, crinkled and dog-eared, reminded Lillian of her true home. She flipped the page to keep it hidden. Mother would take this postcard and tear it into little pieces if she knew this memory existed, and Lillian was learning that sometimes, it was better to hide things than to risk the truth.

༒༒༒

This was not the life she thought they'd have, but oh how it was better than Michigan and working at the Milliken's cleaning up after rich people. Cora had a plan, and if Lillian would just be quiet and amenable, their life would improve. For the first time, Cora was doing what she wanted, what she needed. She was no longer under the thumb of her father, or the wants of John. She was independent, now and could act on impulse if she wanted. And what she wanted was Zeke. Everything revolved around Zeke. He was a Maypole and she danced around him. He liked being at the center of things, she thought, and it was easy to make him be at the center of her.

It turned out that the Garden Room he ran with his uncle, wasn't the entire truth. The Garden Room belonged to his Aunt Mabel, the buxom woman with the bright red hair. He'd been raised in the house, and his uncle might have been any one of the thousands of men who had passed through its doors. In a way, they were all his uncles. His mother had died long ago. She was found floating in the Chicago River. Aunt Mable said she was pushed, but Zeke said he'd always wondered if she'd jumped. It didn't matter. Aunt Mabel treated him like her own. Recently, she'd sent him out on scouting missions to obtain 'new talent'. That's what he was really doing on the ship, although he did work on a sailing ship once in his teens and brought over a load of Christmas Trees. "That's when I was trying to make my own way. It lasted about a week. It was hard work. Fucking hauling trees and all those Germans. I tell you, there's no shame working in a whorehouse. And for a man, it's downright pleasant." He'd laughed then and licked her stomach.

He was a talented man, she thought, and if she could just get him to fall a little more in love with her, he'd change everything. But Cora couldn't be too needy at first. She'd have to let him want to take care of her. Men were like that. Men needed to feel powerful. She'd had years of training to learn that.

She sat at the vanity trying to put up her hair. Her neck was long and lean and if the light wasn't too bright on her, she'd still pass for a girl in her early twenties, and not nearly the thirty that she was. And why shouldn't she be twenty-two again? She could be whoever she wanted to be in Chicago. But the girl. The girl. It was hard to be twenty-two when your child was nearly twelve. She reminded herself that maybe they could be sisters. Sisters was less of a shameful thing. Cora thought, again, of the weight of Lillian and all she represented. Best get her to work and keep her occupied, then Cora could work on Zeke, and the life she wanted would be hers. She'd have perfume and satin, yet. She'd have people wait on her and put up her hair for her. She'd have Zeke to kiss the side of her neck, maybe decorate it with a strand of pearls. She'd have him kiss the bottom of her feet one day, in worship.

❧11❧

They walked for days it seemed. Cora insisted that Lillian stop at every factory door and ask for work, whether there was as sign or not. It was humiliating, but Lillian had no other choice. If she wanted to eat, if she wanted to keep the room at the boarding house, she'd have to find something that paid. She knew without a doubt that her mother was done with working. She was no longer that person. Please, Lillian thought, let me find something quick, and let it not be killing an animal.

They had visited a string of factories that made everything imaginable: rugs, shoes, furniture. No one was hiring. "We'll have to try the meat district then," Mother said. "Zeke says there's always work there."

"Please, Mama, no." Lillian knew she sounded like a child, again. Her feet hurt from walking, and the heat from the sun had caused her body to be slick with sweat. Her brown dress was heavy from her own perspiration. "Maybe we could go back to that nice German house. I could help her at the desk. I could do so many things."

Mother stopped. They were ants in a large city, the building tall around them, carriages hurtling past, swarms of people walking all around them. Threaded among them were the walking skeletons of the hungry. Lillian tried hardest of all not to see them, but sometimes she couldn't help it. Mother pointed to a man picking through slop on the street, looking for food. "Is that what you want for us? You want us to be like that?" Mother turned her face to force Lillian to see. "Open your eyes, because that, Lillian, that is reality. I know you want to go back to your cherry blossoms and your schoolhouse, but that life is over. That man over there, that is what waits for us if you don't do your part."

The words Lillian wanted to say were tiptoeing on her tongue, threatening to flit off, *But what about your part. What are you doing to take care of us?*

Mother looked at her as if she heard the words anyway. "And I am doing my part too. I am. Your father is at the bottom of the lake. He is gone. There isn't anyone to take care of us. I need to find a husband, and my best prospect right now is Zeke. He's got oodles of money so I've got to persuade him. Do you understand? I've got to be at my best. Once I've got him, then we'll be fine, but you're going to have toughen up now, Lillian. I can't work in the factory or he'll smell it on me."

Lillian swallowed the tears and nodded. Oh, how she wished that a woman could take care of herself. If they had stayed in Michigan, maybe Mother could've married Pastor Tom. He would make sour lemonade and give them platitudes about God, but Lillian could've lived with that, she could've loved that.

The thin man across the street scooped something from the street and put it to his mouth, sucking on his fingers. He was so thin Lillian thought that if she were next to him, his skin would be translucent, so thin she'd see the working of his veins, the dark blood coursing through him. "I'll do my best," she said softly, worrying that even her best wouldn't be enough to make her mother love her.

There was a red factory just a few blocks from the boardinghouse they were staying in. Black smoke chugged from its smokestacks and the moaning of cows and steers made the ground vibrate. "This one," Cora said. They'd arrived first thing in the morning, to watch the workers go in. There were men with strong arms, the ones who did the butchering. Women with their hair wrapped in scarves, to keep off the blood. And scores and scores of children. Lillian didn't know what they did but she was afraid. The children looked like dolls, their eyes made of glass.

Cora tapped the shoulder of a short woman and said "Excuse me, please? Miss? My daughter needs work. Can you tell us where to go?"

The woman turned and sneered at them. A deep purple blotch covered half her cheek and ran down her chin.

"I pity you," the woman said. "This place is like working in Hell."

"If it's Hell you want, then see the foreman, over there," another woman joined in and pointed across the stockyard.

Mother nodded and brought a handkerchief up to cover her nose. The stench was so strong it was like a living thing, and Lillian supposed it was. Or the last of living things, the rotten stench of animals' souls forced from their bodies with the punch of a blade.

They pushed their way through the crowd. A bell rang signaling the start of the day. The foreman stood on a platform. He was short and as wide as he was tall. His arms and legs were so solid that he looked like he could crush a steer's skull with his bare hands. "Excuse me, sir?" Cora called. Lillian tried to disappear into herself. "My daughter?"

"What about her?" He looked down at them, judging. "She's a pretty little thing, but I've already got a wife. I could use a mistress, though." And then he laughed, a phlegmy laugh that rattled in his chest.

"She needs work, sir." Mother said, with a little bite to her words. "Is there anything she could do?"

His jaws worked for a moment and then he spit a dark arch of chewing tobacco onto the ground. "C'mere," he said. Lillian looked to Mother who gave her shoulders a little shove. "Lemme see your hands." Lillian climbed up the short staircase to stand before him. He took her tiny hands in his rough meaty ones and turned them over. "You've never done any work at all, have you?" Lillian shook her head. "Well, you'll lose that pretty tender skin soon enough working here. You can collect and clean the eggs. Pays fifty cents a week, if you meet your quota." He bent down and whispered to her "How's that sound to you, little mistress?" He smelled of body odor and onions and meat gone bad. Lillian nodded. It was the only offer of work she had. He slapped her back then and laughed that same sick sounding laugh.

"She can start today. Now, if you want," Mother offered. The foreman nodded.

"I'll come back at the end of the day," Mother said. "Then you'll know the route and can walk yourself. Do as he says." And then she turned and walked off, her hand still to her nose with the kerchief.

"Chester!" The man bellowed. "We've got another young one for you! Take her to the yard."

Lillian's spirit shook, but she tried to steady herself. She must be strong. She must. She must wrap steel threads around her heart to protect her and earn her fifty cents. She envisioned steel cables twirling around her heart, snapping into place, building a fortress around her circulatory system the way that Chicago was rising around her into a monstrous city.

❧❧❧

As Cora left her daughter surrounded by the death moans of cattle and deep in the stench of processing meat, she was not without remorse, but she steeled her heart against it. The world was a tough place. The weak did not survive. With each step away from the factory and farther away from her daughter, she felt equal parts relief and a burgeoning pride. Lillian would have to work hard, and her tender hands would harden, but Cora had saved her from a worse fate. She had saved her from the pumping and grinding that was surely to come if she let John get any closer to her. The way he'd hugged her and carried her had made Cora sick, echoing a mournful song she knew far too well from the sweat of her own father. She had spared Lillian this, and while things were tough, Lillian would be tougher, and they would get through this. Though fifty cents a week was barely enough to keep them fed and housed, they would get by, and Cora would find a way to make up the difference.

She walked on, thoughts of Lillian discarded behind her, like stepping out of an old dress.

Why, in just hours, she was seeing Zeke. He had a business opportunity for her, he'd said. While she'd like that opportunity to be a ring around her finger, she knew that would come. She walked the street, heading toward the Garden Room. The Packinghouse District changed slowly to the Red Light District. Both places sold meat, of a sort, but at least, the Red Light District was festooned with flowers and beauty to cover up the blood and tears.

While walking, she dreamed of Zeke's lips on her. She had never known such pleasure. She had not fully realized that her body was capable of receiving pleasure, having only given it. But after that first night when he had caught her in the shadows of the alley by the Garden Room, and he had whispered, "I want you", she had told him to take her, the need was so great.

"You may be an older woman, Cora," Zeke had joked with her, "But your cunt is a fresh as a girl's." These harsh words from anyone else would have caused her a surge of anger, but instead, it only excited her. Thinking about him, she increased her steps, speeding through the town. She so wished she could get another dress. Take Zeke with her this time to buy her something more appropriate. She'd been so foolish to get this gaudy old thing, but the Irish girl had bedazzled her with talk of moonlight and mystery and how the color would bring out the flash in her eyes.

Cora had learned her lesson.

When she came to the boardwalk, Cora found a bench to sit and wait for Zeke and catch her breath. Out on Lake Michigan, white sails billowed in the July breeze. *Is John out there even now,* she wondered. *Has he let us go?* If she had one regret, it was that a storm hadn't actually carried him to the bottom of the lake. Maybe it if had, she could finally outrun this strange weight that seemed to pull at her, even when she was sitting on a bench, listening to the waves and the city throb around her, feeling happy. Even then, there was an echo of something dark. The rumble of thunder, maybe—but not from the horizon. No. The portent of a storm came from the hollow of her chest.

Cora took a deep breath. There was nothing to fear, she assured herself. Storms always passed, and they never really hurt you.

⚜⚜⚜

Chester was not, as Lillian feared, another giant of a man, stocky and gruff, but a little boy younger than her who was so dirty, his face looked brown, his blue eyes brilliant in the grime. "Another one?" the boy groused.

"Look at her, Chester. She's a cherry. You'll like this one," the foreman said. He grabbed hold of himself between his legs and barked a laugh so fierce that Lillian closed her eyes.

Chester laughed too, trying to copy the same kind of laugh, but from his withered body it came out more like a hiss. "She collectin' eggs or checkin' them?"

The Foreman scratched his chin. "Show her the ropes. Then, I think checking them for now. Less chance of her getting lost and confused with the pigs. Although, I wouldn't mind a thick slice of girl fried in butter."

Lillian hoped he was joking.

"Come on," Chester said, and he jumped off the platform. Lillian couldn't move. Her body would not respond. It was safer if she didn't move. "You a retard or something?," The foreman spat. "Come on!" He shoved her shoulder, and Lillian's feet started to walk down the platform stairs, and behind Chester's quick footsteps.

He ran across the dirt yard, weaving between the workers getting started for the day. "This here's the pig lot," he said motioning. It smelled of feces. The pigs lumbered around, bouncing into each other. Their pink bodies sunburnt and flecked with dried mud. "You'd think pigs are cute and all, but they'll eat anything. Even people. I once saw an arm in the slop. A whole arm!" Chester said this as if it was wonderful. "So you'd better be careful. See them chickens?" He spoke so quickly and changed subjects so abruptly that Lillian was having trouble understanding him. She did not see the chickens at first, but then, like when she'd hunt for morels with her father in the spring, after she saw the first one and turned on her "mushroom eyes" she could see them everywhere. But instead of seeing the brown caps of mushrooms tenting up a bed of leaves, Lillian saw the chickens pecking at the ground beneath the pigs' feet. "They're eatin' the worms," he said. "And whatever else squiggly things they find. Chickens eat the darndest things, too. We keep 'em all throughout here, even in the slaughter area. Maggots," he said and nodded his head, as if the word explained everything.

He started walking, again and motioned her with his grimy hand. Lillian tried to cover her nose by sinking into the collar of her dress, but the stench was everywhere. She couldn't discern if it was the pigs, the cows, the heat, or Chester, himself. But even tucking her nose did no good to block the smell. It was a like she was swimming in it, underwater, with no hope for surfacing. "You're lucky," Chester said. "When I started, I had to collect the eggs. That means you have to go in among the pigs and cattle, find the chickens' nest and grab the eggs. Ya get pecked sometimes. A kid got trampled, once. Probably became pig food after that, I bet. Nothin' goes to waste here. Nothin' at all."

"But I'm not...collecting?" Lillian offered. Her voices was small and scared sounding.

"Nah. Mr. Peters must've taken a shine to you. You get to go right to inspecting. Here." And at last they entered a red brick building. The room was giant and open. Lillian looked at all the children lined up. Some sat in front of flames, holding up eggs. Some carried baskets of eggs and stacked them. Others used rags to clean them off. Lillian started to retch and turned her head to be sick. Chester laughed. "Took ya long enough!" he said. "You lasted longer than I thought. It right stinks, doesn't it? After awhile, you stop smelling it. To me, it smells like the lake." He took a deep breath and hit his chest. "Mmmm. Clean!" Chester winked at her.

"You wanna clean or inspect?"

"I thought I was inspecting?"

"Same difference," he said. "If I was you, I'd clean. Those flames get hot and if you get your hair in it, fllllooooooohm! There goes your hair. Maybe your face too." He smiled wide, and he was missing his front teeth. How old was this boy? Eight? And he seemed so happy here. Lillian didn't understand.

"I'll clean, then."

Chester took her to a table lined with eggs. "Easy as can be," he said. "A little spit and polish, wipe off the shit and blood, set the eggs over there, and you're good to go. But don't break em'. Every one ya break gets de-duct-ted." He announced the word slowly, proud. Lillian nodded and stood behind the table. The eggs were, indeed, covered in gray and white splotches, or blood, or dried feathers. The stench was overpowering. She could taste it. She gagged again, her stomach heaving, but there was nothing left.

"That's a dry heave," Chester said. "You'll be one of those, I guess. Have fun!" He said and scampered off.

Lillian immediately missed him. She looked around her, at the lines and lines of children quickly working around her. They were small and dirty, these children. No one talked or laughed. There was no singing or sounds at all from them. The only sounds were the death cries of cattle outside the doors. Pigs snorting. And feet shuffling.

Feet. Shuffling. Lillian looked to the side of the room, and then the other side. There was a man in each corner, dark and imposing. They each held a bat. She caught the gaze of one, his face pock-marked and tinged with yellow. "Get started," he said and then spit. He hit the bat against the palm of his hand and it made a smacking noise. The girl in front of Lillian flinched. Lillian picked up an egg. She didn't have a rag so she bent and lifted her dress like the girl in front of her. She heaved again, but spit on the egg and began to polish, her dress immediately stained with her suffering.

⚹12⚹

Cora sat limply on the bench, and even though she was in the shade by the water, a layer of sweat clung to her like a second skin. Her dress was glued to her. Her corset dug into her ribs, making it harder to breathe than usual. Sweat was slick between her breasts and between her legs. Her body so moist that she worried she'd lost control of her bladder. She blamed the dress. This dress that only last week had seemed like the start to something wonderful was now something else. She'd been so foolish to trust that Irish shopgirl. The Irish were such liars. Everyone said so. If only Cora had waited a while longer, watched the women of the city, she'd have seen that the fashion wasn't a moldy green dress festooned with dead feathers. Women wore tight skirts at the waist, shirts with frills, and cropped jacket with pearl buttons. She could've looked so smart if she'd only waited. If she'd only known. Now, she looked like a street person. One of those women who stood in front of a doorway, the door open, inviting in strange men in exchange for a fistful of coin. Maybe not even a fistful.

The heat was a hammer against her. She did not know the time, but surely Zeke should've met her by now. The sun was high and shimmery in the cloudless sky. The lake still before her. Ships in the distance did not glide past like they did on windy days. They sat still. Dead calm, they called it. Dead calm was how Cora felt. When Zeke came, maybe he would take her to a restaurant. A place like she'd walked past just this morning with white linen on the table and real crystal glasses. A place where they served you steak so tender it melted in your mouth. Right now, Cora was melting. It felt like her soul was seeping out of her. Where was Ezekiel?

This heat was unbearable. She dreaded going back to her room. It was dark and close, like being inside an asylum. She couldn't relax there. Sometimes, it felt like the walls themselves were breathing.

Her eyes drifted closed. Zeke would come soon. He was just running late. This heat. It slowed everyone down. Horses clomped slower. She could hear the swishing of their tails and the buzzing of flies. The muted cries of gulls in the distance. There was no wind. No wind at all. No relief. Zeke was relief. He would whisk her away, swirl her around on the dance floor, swirl and swirl and swirl until she was sixteen years old again, until she was ten, and nine, and eight, and seven, when she had her mother and nothing had gone wrong in her world. Any moment now, the heat would break, and Zeke would stand before her, shielding her from the sun and everything else that had gone wrong in her life. Any moment. Any…

ᨒᨒᨒ

At seven o'clock, just when the heat broke, and the world darkened, they rang the bells, and the next shift of workers began to shuffle in. Lillian started to head for the door, but a thin girl motioned to her. "You want to get paid, don'cha?" she asked.

Lillian's heart fluttered. She thought she'd be paid at the end of the week. At the end of the work shift was better. She stood in line, waiting for a gaunt man wearing spectacles to hand out coins. It seemed everyone was getting a different amount.

When it was Lillian's turn, she walked up to him and held out her palm. Her hand was flecked with tiny feathers. "And who are you?" The man asked, his voice nasal.

"Lillian March," she said. "I'm…new here."

He looked at a notepad in front of him. "112 eggs cleaned, 20 cracked. Ten cents a day minus…Here." He counted out some coins and placed them in her hand.

"Four cents?" Lillian asked. She could hardly believe it. Four cents wasn't even enough to get a loaf of bread or even a dozen of the eggs she'd polished.

"You want to make money, don't break the eggs. And move faster. Next!" he called.

The boy behind her made ten cents, and Lillian was sick with envy.

Maybe she was just plain sick. Every cell in her body hurt, even her hair. She'd dry heaved most of the day so that her stomach muscles caused a spasm of pain. Her hands were shaking and cramped. She was weak with hunger since Mother had not thought to give her a lunch. Chester had tossed her a roll saying she owed him, but she had trouble keeping it down.

Her only solace was to know the day was done and she could rest. Mother would be waiting for her, and they could walk together. Cora would hold her hand and maybe tuck Lillian in like she used to, lay her hand on Lillian's forehead, brush her hair and coo to her. She'd forgive the four cents. Maybe Zeke had fallen in love with her already, and they could all move back to Traverse City. Or maybe Papa would rise from the grave and rescue them.

Who was she kidding?

Both seemed equally unlikely.

Lillian shuffled along with the other children. The others kept on walking, but Lillian stood at the gate to the stockyard and waited. The effort to remain standing was enormous. Someone bumped into her, and she staggered and fell to her knees in the dirt, her knees skinned raw by the stones on the ground, her four cents tossed out before her. She started to cry then, the tears running and mixing with her sweat. She tried to grab the coins as quickly as she could and hold them tight. They were as slippery as trying to catch minnows with her bare hands. After she found the fourth coin, she tried to get up but couldn't. She didn't have the energy. The yard was nearly empty, and Mother wasn't there.

She would come though, wouldn't she? She'd promised she'd come. But what if…

Lillian didn't want to finish that thought. What if Mother didn't come for her? What if, at long last, the last ties that held them together snapped and Mother swam like a fish broken free from the line. What if Lillian was alone?

"Wha'cha doing on your knees?" a small voice asked, and Lillian knew it was Chester. "You prayin'? No sense of that here. I'm born and raised here, and God ain't ever heard a single word I've uttered, not even the bad ones. You oughtta get up."

"I can't," Lillian said, sniffling.

"Do it anyway," Chester said, as if it was easy. Maybe for him it was. "You don't get up, you're as good as pig feed." He bent down and whispered, his words a burst of heat on her neck and ear. "I'm not joking. I wish I was."

He stood up and kicked her, not hard, but maybe if people were watching they wouldn't know that. "Get up," he said.

Lillian used her hands to push herself up and stood slowly, swaying like a cattail in the breeze, though the wind here was still.

"Now get out," he said. "You want to work tomorrow, you gotta be strong. And bring something to eat. To make it here, you gotta learn fast." He smiled at her then, his toothless grin both young and old at the same time.

"My mother isn't here to pick me up," Lillian said, but Chester had already faded into the crowd.

How long should she wait? What if the foreman saw her? What if the men with the bats caught her? Dark would fall soon, and then what would happen? Would the next shift confuse her with a pig? Would they gut her and hang her upside down?

Lillian's feet were moving slowly and before she knew it she was doing a half-run half-limp. She knew the way back to the boarding house where she could sleep and get strong. She'd find food. She'd do what she'd have to. And Mother would find her. She would. Lillian was sure of it.

She stopped thinking then. She just walked, one step at a time, forward.

༄ ༄ ༄

When Cora awoke, her neck was stiff. The shadows had shifted while she slept, and she could already feel the telltale sting of sunburn on her face. What time was it? Her stomach growled. Certainly lunch was long past. Where was Zeke? She must find him! Maybe something had happened to him. Something dreadful. People in Chicago were injured or maimed in the most gruesome ways: they fell in front of a speeding trolley, they were kicked by an angry horse, bricks from constructions sites could fall on a passerby and squash their heads like a thumb pushing open the skin of an overripe peach.

She forced herself to stand. She was so hungry. There was no money left in her purse. It was pointless to even carry it around with her, but she didn't want anyone to know. Women were always watching, always judging. She couldn't very well walk around without a purse or people would think she was destitute, or even worse, a beggar.

She tried to get her bearings. Everything looked the same: Lake Michigan stretched out wide in front of her, the city behind her, both directions. And where was she to go? If Zeke was hurt, it could've happened anywhere. The only thing to do was to go to The Garden Room and ask.

She walked, though it felt more like a stumble. Her throat was dry and her skin pinched. She needed some water in this heat. Maybe he wasn't hurt or maimed. Maybe she'd misunderstood their plans. But hadn't he said I'll meet you at the wharf? We'll get lunch or something. We'll take a stroll. He had said that, and his lips had quirked up, and Cora thought *those lips have been all over me. Those lips have shown me love.* "We'll take a stroll," he'd said, and Cora had nodded, fluttered her lashes just because.

She had wanted to take a stroll. It sounded refined, like what courting people did. And weren't they courting? Wasn't her suffering going to end soon? It was all just a test of her love for Zeke. She'd pass it. She must.

She walked.

෨෨෨෨

If Lillian believed in God, she would've thanked him for getting her to the boarding house. Instead, she thanked her poor Papa for teaching her to always know where she was headed. "Check where the sun is," he'd said. "It'll tell you where you are and where you need to go."

The sun was setting, but it was okay. She was home. Well, it didn't feel like home, but it was home, for now. She'd used her four cents to buy a slice of ham and a pickle from the Jewish delicatessen on the corner.

The nice German woman, Marta, greeted her warmly when she stumbled in. "You goot girl to help your mother," she'd said. "Children must help their families."

In the room, Lillian dutifully cut the slice of ham and the pickle in half and set one half aside for mother. After a moment, she sliced a little extra ham from Mother's portion to stow away for tomorrow. She would need to be strong if she wasn't going to drop any eggs, and she was determined not to drop a single one. She ate the ham and pickle quickly, the saltiness making her lips pucker.

She slipped out of her dress, folded it neatly on a chair and tried to wash up as best she could. She could still smell the chicken feces on her. It had seeped into her pores. She scrubbed as best she could, then sat on the mat in the corner and picked up her book.

The section was on Walking-sticks, those curious bugs that looked like twigs until you saw them move. She read, "During daylight these walking-sticks must be in constant danger of execution by birds, and presumably it is to escape such danger that they rest so quietly in one position for hours at a time."

It felt like she was reading advice.

༺❀༻❀༺

Chester had followed the girl. There was something about her. Something he couldn't put into words and didn't try to. Anyway, he had no where to go. He slept on the streets, in dark corners if he could find one and hoped that he could sleep without getting buggered. So far, Chester had been lucky, but he didn't think that luck would hold. Luck never did.

He followed the girl. She was tired and moved slow, but he thought she might make it. She had grit to her and that was good. That's what a person needed. There was still something soft about her and he thought, maybe, he'd watch over her a bit, just so she could keep that tiny little spot tender.

Everyone should have a soft spot that they guarded like a pearl. Chester thought maybe the girl would be his.

༺❀༻❀༺

At night, the Garden Room had the allure of a party filled with revelers. It had an aura of mystery and magic, of good people doing bad things. But now, before night had fallen, and the sun was still bright, everything looked tired and sad. Lillian made it to the door, where Franz stood guard. "Girls go in the back entrance," he grumbled.

"I'm not...one of the girls..." Cora said, shocked. She'd been here a handful of times. Shouldn't they know that she and Zeke were courting? That she was his potential wife and not one of those harlots?

"Huh," he grunted, as if not convinced.

"I'm here to see Zeke? My Zeke," she added.

"Oh, right," he said, as if he was remembering the punch line to a joke. "I remember you now. Go on in."

He had, at least, the decency to open the door for her.

The place was near deserted. No piano music played, this time. There was no drunken laughter or giggles. And thankfully, Cora did not have to deal with the imposing figure of Mama Mabel. She just wanted to see Zeke. And then she did, at least the back of him. He was sitting in the salon, the top of his hair visible above the green velvet of the chair. He wasn't moving and Cora had an awful premonition that he was dead. She rushed forward, somehow finding some source of energy deep within her. "Zeke!" she cried.

But he was not dead. No. He was most certainly alive. As was the young girl who was on her knees in front of him, moving quickly up and down his rigid member. "Zeke?" Cora asked, though she knew it was him. It was more that she wanted to know why he was doing this? Why did he need this poor girl when Cora would love him that way if he only asked?

He said nothing, and that was maybe the worst of it. He did not apologize or push the girl away from him. He raised a finger as if to tell Cora to wait, and then placed his other hand on the brunette's bobbing head to move her even faster and deeper and then...he released. In front of Cora. And she knew then, knew with every fiber in her being that she had, once again, created a fantasy around an unworthy man. He did not love her. He had no intention of marrying her. He never had.

After a moment he turned to her. "What do you *want?*" he said, disgusted or annoyed, or maybe both.

Cora collapsed.

❧13❧

Lillian had left the windows open to let in cool air, but it never seemed to cool. She was in an oven and dreamed fitfully of a witch trying to cook her whole. She woke with dawn and the sounds of the street outside her window. Inside the boarding house, a baby was crying, and a man and a woman were yelling at each other. Then there was a sound of a meaty slap, and the woman stopped yelling. Lillian worried that she should run for the police, but then she heard the man stomp off and the woman's muffled cries, so she knew she was still alive. When she lived in Traverse City, the morning noises were so different. She could hear the gentle lapping of the bay, the lonely song of the loon out in the water, mourning doves cooing. Now, the sound of violence was her morning song.

It was dawn, and Mother was not here, her bed still the same as it was last night. Lillian rose, pulled on her soiled dress, looked out the windows, but in the growing mass of tired people gathering outside to walk to their various jobs, she did not see the metallic shimmer of her mother's mossy dress. Lillian looked at the small wooden table, the one where the half of a pickle and small slice of meat sat. She quickly grabbed the small bundle, opened it and shoved both the pickle and the ham into her mouth and chewed, swallowing quickly, her obligation to her mother be damned. She wiped her chin with the back of her hand, head averted to avoid Marta's gaze (she'd know about the food), and then left the room, determined to get to work early, praying that she didn't break a single egg.

Mother would come back. She would. She would come back because their bond was strong. She would be waiting for her tonight.

Lillian did not imagine her mother would hug her or have a pie ready for her, or any other such childish nonsense. Maybe the idea of a bond was childish, too. Still, Mother would be back. She just imagined that her mother had grown tired of being out all night, and would come back to her because there was nowhere else for her to go.

☙☙☙

It was an effort to open her eyes. As a girl, Cora had seen the dark thread that sewed her dead mother's eyes shut, and she'd panicked for a moment thinking that she was dead and she would never open her eyes, again. But they did open. Wherever she was, it was bright and blurry. Two shapes stood over her. One tall and one short and round. Then voices filtered in, but she couldn't understand. It was like swimming underwater and trying to hear someone calling to you. She could hear sounds, but the letters didn't click together to form actual words. And then that changed, too, and she surfaced.

"Drink this," the woman said. Cora looked, focused, and could see the red red hair, the cheeks cracked with age and dried makeup.

"Auntie…" she breathed.

"I'm only Auntie to little Zeke, here. My girls call me Mama Mabel, so I guess you can call me that too. But never just Mama. We don't want to confuse people. I have a reputation to uphold. I ain't nobody's mother." Mama Mabel laughed, and her huge belly and voluminous breasts shook under her red dress. "Drink, girl. Don't make Mama Mabel mad."

Cora didn't want to see this woman mad. If Satan had a wife, she'd probably look like Mama Mabel. Cora drank. She'd thought it was water, but it was bitter and burned her throat. She sat up and coughed and coughed.

"What kind of women are you fucking, Zeke? She can't even handle a bit of Laudanum? This woman needs to toughen up. Maybe you should *spank* her." Mama Mabel's laughter continued, rolling along with the fat of her stomach, following her out of the room.

Cora cleared her throat and looked around. She was in Zeke's room, again, and the laudanum made her feel immediately relaxed and…smoothed out. Like her sharp edges had suddenly been rounded with sand paper. She felt lovely. "Can I have some more of that?" she asked softly.

"Not if you don't want to pass out, again." Zeke moved the glass out of her reach. "You fainted, you know. You sick or something? Or just crazy?" He was smiling at her, but it was a snake's smile.

"I'm not sick," Cora said, though she wasn't entirely sure that was true. She didn't feel right. She was weak and hot and hungry. "Or crazy," she added. "You were late, and I was…I think I needed something to drink. Or eat. I waited all day for you."

"Huh. Waited for me? Why?"

"Because you'd said…" Cora began.

Zeke chuckle. "You're a glutton aren't you? You're one of those women that likes to suffer. It's a shame you're so old, Cora. If you were ten years younger…the fun we'd have." He slapped his knee. Cora couldn't quite understand him. Didn't they have fun? Weren't they going to have more fun? Wasn't he falling in love with her? What was happening?

"Look," he said. "I get it. I get that you adore me or what have you, but you've got to get it through your head. We're never going to be more than what we are. You get that? I mean, that alleyway was fun, and the next night you were here and offered and…what can I say? I like a free snack every now and then. But I don't have any kind of agreement with you, you understand? You get that."

Cora didn't move or breathe. Her vision blurred suddenly.

"I can tell you're hungry. You're skinny as a fence post. So…two screws, that right?"

"Screws?" Cora had no idea what he was talking about. Screws? Fence posts?

"I'll give you two bucks. That's more than you'd get on the streets." He tossed two bills at her. "Now, I don't owe you anything, you get that? We're square. And once you can get on your feet, you need to get on out of here."

Cora looked around again. The room was bright. Light filtered in through the window, pouring across the bed and illuminating the wallpaper. It was striped. Green stripes. There were pictures of birds covering one wall entirely. They were of all sizes and shapes, in a rainbow of colors. They looked hand-drawn. Their frames ran into one another. Why had she never noticed that before? It was so bright, but when she'd gotten here it had been dark so that meant…

"My daughter!" she cried, remembering suddenly that she'd forgotten to pick up Lillian.

Zeke shook his head, a smile on his lips. "Ah, so that's it, is it? You're a surprise, ain't ya? Here I thought you were thinking we were sweethearts, but that's not at it at all. Your daughter. She's a cherry, surely?" He didn't wait for her to answer. "I'll give you a hundred dollars for her."

Cora didn't understand. "What?"

"You're a mean one, huh? Maybe I should give you one more go after we negotiate." He lifted her skirts, ruffling the fabric, slipped his hand under her bloomers and immediately found her mound with his hot hand. He started moving his fingers against her. He struck something between her legs, and Cora moaned even though she didn't want to. He focused his finger on that single point, circling round and round. "Two hundred dollars. No more than that. That's a fair price. Better than fair. And that's more than you'd make in three, maybe four years."

He slid his finger inside her and Cora's head fell against the pillow. If only she could stay here forever and ever in this room, her edges smoothed, his finger delving in and out of her. She'd never felt such pleasure. It was a wonder her body was capable of such glory. How had she never known this? The birds on the wall shivered and began to flap their wings, about to take flight. Something started to quicken within her as he pulsed his fingers. He leaned down, his lips a feather's breadth from her own, and then, without understanding or wanting, something happened to Cora. Her body tensed and flooded with pleasure.

His fingers instantly stilled.

Cora saw the stars.

He withdrew his hand, smoothing her rumpled dress and then licked his fingers.

"Two hundred dollars," he said, finality in his voice. "Drop her off, and I'll give you your money. After that, I don't want to see you, again."

Cora—limp, exhausted, confused, and buzzing with pleasure—nodded.

❧❧❧❧❧

"Hullo, Cherry!" Chester called to her. She could recognize his voice, even without seeing the dirty face standing before her, his smile big and gap-toothed.

"How did you know that I lived by a cherry orchard?" she asked. They were walking to the building that housed the eggs. Chester was walking with her until he found something that needed to be done".

"Cherry orchard?" He clearly didn't understand what she meant. Then he started laughing. He laughed so hard he stopped walking and started slapping his knee over and over. "That's a knee slapper, that is!" And he slapped it again. "Don't you know what a cherry is?"

Of course she knew. "A fruit," she said. Just two months ago, her fingers were stained by the juice of them. She thought the deep purple would never come out.

"A fruit!" he said and laughed again. "A cherry is a girl that ain't even been mounted, like the cows mount each other. People aren't much different from animals. I see 'em mount all the time." Suddenly, he stopped laughing and reached for her hand. "Come on," he said, but he whispered it and Lillian could see that he was frightened. They started running then and ran all the way to the open red brick building and the eggs and the feathers and the air thick with sweat and stink and shit and blood.

"What's...wrong?" They'd run so hard that she could barely breathe.

Chester looked at her and his brown eyes watered. When he spoke next, he spoke quickly and with a voice that lacked all mirth. "Watch yourself, Lillian. The foreman likes you, and it's never good to be liked. I should know. I'll call you Cherry in front of him and all the other men because it makes them laugh. You do what you have to here to survive, and I've done plenty." He wiped his eyes quickly with the back of his hand and then started to run off. He turned and shouted: "Get to work, Cherry! Drop and egg and I'll be the first to clobber ya!"

Lillian nodded, and went inside to take her place at the table and clean the eggs quickly and gently. She felt the tears in the back of her throat, how they swelled like the bay when it was angry, but they didn't surface. The men in the corner watched her, and she knew then what they were. Wolverines, waiting for the right moment to pounce.

She picked up an egg and polished it with the edge of her dress, while her mind thought of getting a small piece of steel, something that she could polish at night and make it gleam, and then tuck it into the sleeve of her dress. Her father had taught her to gut a fish, and if a man tried to mount her, she figured she could gut him, too.

By the end of the morning, all the eggs in front of her were cleaned of filth, and she hadn't broken a single one.

Lillian was a fast learner.

Oh, the wind was lovely on her face and running through her hair and kissing her neck. "It tickles!" Cora sighed happily.

The cab jostled over the pock-holed street, and came to a sudden stop.

"This is as far as I'll go, lady. No point going into the Packinghouse District. You're all dirt poor over there. No one will be able to afford to hire me outta here." Zeke had already paid the driver to carry her away from him. Zeke was a prince, and this was her coach, and Cora wanted to dance and dance and dance. She tried to step lightly out of the car, but her ankle landed wrong, and she twisted, landing in the muck. Muck was lovely, though. It was soft and slippery. "Sssslippery," she said. What a funny word. She sat there giggling, barely noticing that the coach had pulled off and she was all alone.

Nothing looked familiar, and everything was new. "Stinks," she said and tried to stand. Her foot wasn't working right. There was no pain, though, and she was floating and weightless, but it took her a few tries to stand. The houses here were no better than shacks, but everything looked soft and glowy to her. She began to walk, and that made her giggle, too. One foot was fine, but the other made her hunch to the left with every step. "I'm training to be a hunchback!" she cried, and she liked the words on her lips. "Hunch. Back." She said again and licked her lips. Her lips were lovely. The world was lovely. It would be lovelier still when she found her way back home and she could sleep. Really, that was all she wanted. A good, long sleep.

She shuffled forward, tall and then hunched, tall and then hunched.

It took her forever to find the slouching boardinghouse, but she eventually made it. The soft glow of the laudanum was fading, and her ankle hurt. Her body hurt. She was one big ache. In the doorway, Mr. Andersson waited. He smelled of onions and warm sweat. "Rent's due tomorrow," he said.

Cora nodded and fluttered her hand. "Rent, rent," she said. She tried to pass him, but he wouldn't budge.

He leaned into her and inhaled deeply. "You're pretty as a flower, but you still smell like the same shit as everyone else around here. You pay the rent first thing in the morning, or you'll pay in another way."

He stayed close to her. She did not look at him but focused on his open shirt, the coarse hair on his chest, the acne bumps. "I can pay," she said. "Tomorrow."

He smiled and stepped aside, gesturing like he was allowing her to enter a palace.

Cora slowly climbed the stairs. The air was thick around her. Dark. Hot. Sleep called to her. She wanted to slip under, burrow into the dark and never wake up.

She opened the door. The room was empty. Her foot hurt. She shuffled to the bed, crawled into it, and let the black wash over her like a dark wave.

❧❧❧

Lillian made a dime at the end of the day. A whole ten cents. She smiled to herself. "Better tuck it away," Chester whispered in her ear, startling her. He seemed to have a knack for jumping up unexpectedly. "There's folks here that'll take that from you."

She knew he wasn't joking. She coughed and bent down to adjust her shoe, and slip the coin into it. She could feel it against her skin. When she stood, Chester was still there. "Why are you helping me?" she asked.

"Dunno." He rubbed his nose. There was a strand of dried snot running from his nose to his lip. "Maybe you remind me of my sister," he said.

"Where's your sister?" Lillian asked. She was afraid to hear his answer. Chester, though smiling brightly, was a very dark soul. "Is she…gone?" she asked. Chester didn't have parents, so to hear he had a sister was a shock.

"Nah. She probably wishes she was. When Ma died, Pap dropped her off at a brothel. Got paid a whole bunch for her, too. Then he took off, and I ended up here." Chester started humming then and doing a little dance, his boots fluffing up the dirt. "It's all a sad, sad song." He sang it like it was a happy thing. He stopped dancing. "She had eyes like yours," he said.

"Brown?"

"No." He scratched his nose again. "Sad. I like sad girls the most."

Then he took off running.

Lillian hoped she'd see him tomorrow. He was the only bright thing in her day. The dime in her shoe was a bright thing, though, too. It meant she'd eat tonight, and if Mother was there, she'd see how hard Lillian was working to rescue them. That would mean something to her. And maybe if Lillian worked very hard for the next few months, she could save enough to get them back across the lake, up into the hills, and nestled in before the cherry trees blossomed, again.

❧14❧

John March hoisted the rucksack filled with clothes, extra food, and a few mementos on his shoulder and walked out of his home, shutting but not locking the door behind him. There was no need. His house now matched how he felt: hollow. There was the small kitchen table, scratched and worn. A glass jar with a dead butterfly and brown grass sat at the center of the table. And there was the counter where Cora rolled pie dough, her arms flexing, her long hair in a bun but coming unraveled, wisps falling into her eyes. There was the chair where John had pulled Cora onto his lap and kissed her fiercely, with a passion he thought she'd matched.

There were the empty pots and pans, the glass jars, the window looking out into the woods and the stretch of the blue bay far off in the distance. And there was Lillian's room, her bed, still unmade. Her stack of books waited for her. John and Cora's room waited, too. A brown dress hung on a nail on the wall. John realized for the first time how ugly it was. How ugly everything was. While he'd scrimped and saved for their future, he'd let his wife and daughter run around in rags. Let their hands roughen with hard work. He had not treated them tenderly.

John wasn't sure how long they'd been gone. Maybe they'd left not soon after he'd gone on the fishing schooner. It took him just a day to prepare to leave this life behind, too—this house, and all it held. He sold what he could. There wasn't much. The Millikens quickly found another young family to move into the place and gave him a few bills for the contents. At the fishery, Mr. Welch didn't even purse his lips at John letting him know he'd be leaving and asking for his final pay. He'd nodded and then hired another man to take on John's duties of gutting and filleting fish.

How quickly they were all replaced—him, Cora, and Lillian—as if they'd never been important in the first place.

If his heart wasn't already broken, that thought might have done it. His heart, though brittle as a dried crayfish, kept beating. He walked past the stable, the wet smell of horse heavy in the air. Past the Milliken's grand house and the long porch where he could still see Cora on her knees, scrubbing.

He walked down the dirt path and through the woods of green maple and ash trees, and into the small cherry orchard. There were no blooms and the fruit had already been harvested. They were just trees now, and Lillian did not wait for him with a handful of bugs to go over, or a section in her biology book she wanted to ask him about.

John found a rhythm to his gait and imagined that somewhere Lillian's heart beat at the same pace.

He didn't know where they were, exactly, but he had enough of an idea. He'd talked to Pastor Tom and he'd mentioned something about a ship docking, and men who worked in Chicago. And there was the newspaper with the circled advertisement. And where else would they go and be able to disappear? They were somewhere in Chicago, then, and had been there for nearly a month, now. If only he hadn't taken that trip. They could've done without the extra money. The cherry orchard dream. If only. If only Cora had loved him more. And maybe now there was some anger coursing through him, propelling him forward the way a strong wind would. Maybe he was angry at Cora for being so in her head. For not being the kind of woman he'd thought she was. For not loving him enough. Or even at all.

Pastor Tom had mentioned Cora talking to a young man at the picnic, a sailor. The man had talked to a few of the young women in town who'd smartly turned away from him. "There was something slimy about that man," Pastor Tom said. "Something like a snake. He talked to Cora for some time, you know. Longer than a young man should talk to a married woman." Pastor Tom had wanted to say more, but John held up his hand to stop him. He didn't need to hear any more. His father had been right. He'd known all along that he would never be enough for her. Never handsome enough, or rich enough, or interesting enough to keep a woman like Cora tied to him. He'd known it all along but thought he could change her mind. What a fool he'd been.

As he walked, he tried to set aside his personal hurt. This was not that time to be soft. This was a time to be fierce. He was used to hard work. His hands showed the years of it. His body was strong and lean and well-muscled. He'd walk all the way to Chicago if he needed to. Swim across Lake Michigan. He'd do whatever he had to find her.

It wasn't Cora he was looking for, but his Lillian. Cora was lost to him. Now, he knew the truth. She had never been his in the first place.

He walked. The sun hot on his shoulders, burning the back of his neck. He tried to feel the beat of his daughter's heart with his own, to quiet himself enough that maybe he could hear it. High in the trees, a cicada shrilled. He thought, maybe, she was calling for him. He picked up the pace. He imagined hearing his daughter's voice. She called "Papa! Papa!" over and over to him until the words shifted and changed, becoming one long high-pitched cry. What made him move faster was that she said his name with such fear. He dropped the rucksack to the ground and started running.

Now that he'd sold everything, the only thing he really needed was the little bit of money he had left.

Everything else was just extra weight holding him down.

❧15❧

Cora couldn't get up. She couldn't. The bed had invisible ties binding her down. She could twist and roll over, but the idea of getting out of bed, of moving her feet to touch the wood floor, of doing anything at all, was beyond abhorrent. It was physically impossible.

"Mother?" Lillian asked softly. Cora's skin prickled, this time not at the sound of her daughter's voice, but at her daughter's stench.

Cora moaned. Even words were too much. "It's too bright," she managed. "Turn down the light."

"It's the sun, mother. It's dawn. I'm late. If I don't get to the factory…"

"Then what are you waiting for? Just go!" She was so exhausted. Even her blood hurt. She could feel it sluggish in her body. Her brain pounded. She wanted the darkness and silence of sleep. She wanted everything to go away. Her daughter. Zeke. This room. She wanted Chicago to burst into flames, to burn to a black crisp and collapse in a heap of ashes, her useless body along with it. She wanted to be numb.

"All right, Mother. I've left you some bread. And here is what I've earned the last few days. It's not much but I'm getting better. Some kids make as much as forty or fifty cents a day! I'll get there. I promise."

Lillian laid the coins on Cora's chest. They felt heavy as an iron brick. She couldn't breathe. She waited until she heard Lillian shuffle out the door—would the girl never pick up her feet?—until she opened her eyes and counted the paltry coins. It was time to pay the rent and she did not have enough. She would be over a dollar short, and that Mr. Andersson would come calling.

Let him call, she thought. Let everyone call. She'd just lie here and try to slip out of her body for a while. She's slip into the black. She closed her eyes. The light dimmed. The dark was so much easier on her spirit.

≈≈≈

Lillian walked quickly to work, skirting around the people in the congested streets. It was already a scorching day, as if standing before a fire. They were in the worst of summer now and Lillian prayed that this heat would last only a day or two. Afraid of being late, she started to run. "Watch it, ya wench!" a burly man said when she ran into him and stumbled. She quickly backed up and then ran around him. If she was late and she lost her job, then what would happen to them? She didn't let her imagination run with that horror. There were too many possibilities.

Instead, she focused on her body moving. She imagined herself as an ant, scurrying forward in search of food, so strong that she could carry ten times her own weight. If only that were true. It was taking all of her energy to get to the factory in time.

When she neared the stockyard, she came to an abrupt stop, her chest heaving with the effort to breathe, to soothe her lungs from working so hard. There were throngs of people out of the gates, and the stockyard was empty. The cows cried louder than usual, and the heat was so intense that she could feel it curling the fine hairs in her nose. "What's happening?" she asked, not really to anyone in particular, since everyone here was a stranger to her.

A thin women with her hair wrapped in a scarf looked down at her. "'Tis a fire," she said, her voice lilting the way the Irish did. Mother didn't like the Irish, but Lillian thought their speech was a kind of music. "There was an explosion. They'll be carrying out the bodies soon."

"If they can find them," a man said and laughed. "I felt that explosion in my bones, didn't you? They'll be lucky to find parts."

"But what about..." Lillian felt guilty for asking, but she was already feeling the dull throb of hunger and worried about going back home without any money. "What about our work?"

"Oh, they'll be no work today. Not for the lot of us."

"Get out of they way!" A man's voice yelled and the crowd and Lillian parted, squeezing so close to each other that their sweaty bodies touched. A stream of firemen spilled forward. "You! Men! Help us now, would you? We've got buckets."

Lillian didn't hear what he said after that because there was another explosion and a blast of heat so fierce that it pushed Lillian back.

She heard crying then and screams. She could see the flames now, and the air was heavy with the scent of roasting meat. Lillian was ashamed, because it smelled good.

The throng of people was so dense around her that she could not see. They were men and women who were much taller than she was. "There they are!" someone said. The crowd surged forward. Lillian wiggled between the people until she reached the front of the iron bars of the stockyard. Men stumbled out of the smoke, their faces black with soot. Two men dragged another between them, his arms wrapped limply around their shoulders. Another man cradled the limp body of a child in his arms.

"Chester," Lillian breathed. She couldn't be sure. She couldn't see him closely enough in the smoke. Then someone shoved her out of the way, back into the crowd, and she couldn't see anything at all.

❧❧❧

There was a pounding in her brain. It echoed off the insides of Cora's skull. Then the sound seemed to come from the outside instead of from within her body. The door. Someone was at the door.

"Rent's due, missy!"

It was Andersson bellowing, Andersson banging his meaty fist against the door, Andersson who smelled of onions and sweat and underneath it all, that bitter bite of anger. Cora moaned and covered her eyes. She would ignore him. If she ignored him, he would go away like a good man and let her sleep. What she wanted more than anything was to be left alone in peace and quiet, and just sleep. When she slept, she was able to escape. She didn't think about Chicago, or the money she'd lost getting here. She didn't think of her little house in Traverse City and how she couldn't just shut her mouth and be happy with what she had. She didn't think of Zeke. Zeke and how much she still wanted him, of her pinned against the wall, lifted by his muscles, while he pounded into her so mercilessly that she felt buoyed by the pain. She didn't think of the embarrassment of what was true: he did not love her. He did not love her because she was old. She offered nothing useful to him. When she slept, all of this slipped away like holding water in her palm.

The pounding stopped.

Thank god. He'll go now. He is a good man, and he will go.

And then she heard the key turning in the lock.

"Had a late night, huh, missy?" Andersson asked. She could smell him all the way across the room. Today, he had the added stench of bell peppers. She hated bell peppers. They overpowered everything they touched. He walked into her room. "Time to get up, don'tcha know?" He walked over to the curtains, throwing them open. Cora's eyes squeezed shut but still couldn't block out the brightness. "It's lunchtime, and you're still sleeping. Maybe you work at night, huh?" he said, and then sat on the end of the bed, next to her feet. She felt the bed sink with his heft. "Hey," he said. "Hey. Look at me."

She struggled to open her eyes and sit up. When she sat up, she realized she was only wearing a flimsy sheath, the shape of her heavy breasts clear beneath. She clenched the blanket to her chest, but it was too late. The way he licked his lips made it clear he'd already seen. "It's rent day," he said. "Rent." He tasted the word.

"I have money," she said, thankful that Zeke had tossed her those bills. She grabbed them from the beside table and held them out to Mr. Andersson.

He leaned over, resting his hand on her leg for balance. "One. Two," he said, plucking the bills from her hand. "That's two bucks. Rent is four. It's four dollars a week, not two." He smiled, and he looked like a fish. All those tiny teeth.

"It was two dollars last month."

"Last month, I had a deal with Zeke. He puts his women up here, but when he's done with them, the rent goes back up. Now it's four."

"I only have two," she said. She'd stopped breathing. Ages ago, maybe. Maybe she'd die right there in bed, his hand slowly moving up her leg, pushing up her flimsy sheath.

"Well, now, I'm a reasonable fella. I'm a businessman, and there's no reason why you and me can't come up with some kind of our own arrangement." His hand gripped her leg, and she braced herself for what she knew was coming next. "We can go twice to pay it off, or once. But if it's once, then it's the way I want it, and no questions and no funny stuff from you. So. That's the deal. You want it once? Or twice?"

Cora longed for some of that bitter laudanum. She'd floated away with just a drink. It was better than sleep. Better than dreams. Better than death, because death was permanent. She didn't want permanent. She just wanted to float away for a while. Once. Or twice. It was a simple question. Did she let him take her two times and have to endure his stench and weight longer, or did she surrender and hope that it would be over soon? She did what she always did with men. Surrender was the easy choice. Just get it over with.

"Once," she said.

He nodded and smiled, as if he'd been hoping for that answer.

He stood, and Cora could already tell he was excited by her. She closed her eyes and kept them closed tight as he grabbed her, flipped her over, shoved up her dress, tore at her, and made her pay for her rent.

❧❧❧

Lillian tried to push through the crowd to see, to know for sure, but they were no better than cattle, and moving was impossible. She couldn't see him. She couldn't find him. And the men carrying him out were already gone. "Come back tomorrow!" A voice boomed. "Factory's closed, today!"

"What about our pay?" Another voice called.

"You didn't do any work today, did ya? Come back tomorrow, and see if you still have a job. All of you! Get!"

The crowd moved slowly, breaking apart like ice floes in Lake Michigan. Lillian felt herself being swept away. What did it matter if it was Chester or not? She shouldn't have cared so quickly. She shouldn't have cared at all. When you cared, that's when you were at danger. That's when Nature swept in and reminded you that life was not a fairground filled with laughter and cotton candy. Life was a brutal forest where only the cruel survived.

Maybe she should learn to be cruel.

۞۞۞

"Excuse me, but have you seen a mother and a daughter traveling together? About a month ago? Maybe longer?" Was there any other string of words more pointless to utter to passing strangers on a busy dock? How many thousands of people had passed by the water between the time he lost them and arrived in Chicago. Who would remember a girl and mother? Even now, John could see dozens and dozens of women walking together. They were separate, in pairs, in groups, pushing strollers, quietly talking, walking arm in arm. They did not look him in the eye but looked down, and they blurred together. How could he possibly find Cora and Lillian in such a sea of women?

But he asked the questions, again and again, to anyone who would stop to listen. He held the only portrait he had, his wedding picture, he and Cora staring into the camera, Cora seated in front of him, him posed behind her, his hand on her shoulder. They did not smile. And the picture did not capture Cora's spirit. It was the picture of a body, not a person. But he still asked.

"Have you seen her?"

"Did you meet a woman who…"

"Excuse me…sir…ma'am…"

"The girl, she's about this tall, she reads. She had a book on insects…"

"Do you remember…"

And if they answered him it was a variation of the same: no. No. No. A shake of the head. Don't bother me. Piss off.

But he kept asking. Again and again and again. He stayed on the dock for two days without rest, asking and asking. Until… "*Ja*," the man in the carriage said. He was bigger than John, and bald. "A girl with her mother." His accent was thick and Slavic. John knew a handful of German. It helped on the ships.

"*Entschuldigung,*" John said. Excuse me. "*Bitte. Wo?*" Please. Where?

The man smiled at him. "English is okay," he said. "Is Chicago, no? I do not know where they are, but I know where they went. Come with me. I will take you there. There is good food and a place to sleep. Good room. Good food. It looks like maybe you need a bit of both."

John nodded and climbed inside the cab.

༺༚༚༚

Andersson finished his business with a shudder and a grunt. He kissed the back of her neck, withdrew, tucked himself away and left, locking the door behind him. Cora lay there. For hours.

Her spirit was a tenuous thing, and she held on to her grief for as long as she could. It felt like years since they'd left Traverse City and boarded the train and then the ferry. Who was she back then? She was not this woman, the one who lifted her dress and closed her eyes and offered her flesh so that she had a place to sleep. She was not this woman, whose daughter went off to work before the sun rose and came back after the sun had set, smelling of eggs and rot. Who was this woman with the knobby hands and snarled hair? Who had a sweaty man's seed seeping from between her legs and did nothing about it. Who wore this shiny green and orange dress looking more like a harlot than a fashionable lady. Surely it wasn't her. But it was. Her hands, her dress, her laying on bed while Mr. Andersson sweated over her.

She was no lady. Not anymore. And if she was being honest with herself, she was never a lady. She'd never even had the chance.

And the worst of it was, that in all honesty, she didn't mind so terribly much anymore. For two months, she'd been living in a lovely sort of haze.

When Lillian left for the day, Cora existed in a happy ether of her own imagination. One where she danced and laughed and floated. All it took was a little bitter drink, and she was outside of her body and younger and beautiful and had everything she wanted. She was happy and loved and warm and safe. Zeke came to her in a dream. "I've been such a fool," he said, grasping at her dress with his smooth hands. His face was streaked with tears because his love for her was so strong. "I love you. I've loved you since the moment I saw you. You're all I think about." Then Zeke pleasured her with kisses and made her body sing alive, again.

But when the bitter drink faded, Cora slammed back down into her cold shell of a body and felt all the sharp points of existing. She was overwhelmed by light and noises, the stench of Chicago and the slaughterhouses just down the street. She couldn't bear to look at Lillian. Her child's face, still soft and hopeful, still tentative when she said to her "Mother, I made a quarter today. A whole quarter!" And God help her if Lillian reached out to touch her. Lillian's touch, her tender fingers, were like needles thrust into her skin.

Cora wanted to float outside it all, and it was only when she was alone in the room, the blinds drawn, the room stifling, and the air unmoving, only then could she relax and forget for a while.

And still, this was better than the life she'd had with John in Michigan. This was, at least, something of her choosing.

That was the thought, that this was a life of her choosing, that finally made her cry. Her body shuddered, and the tears came, and she could not control any of it.

❧❧❧

Auntie Mabel thudded into Zeke's room, shaking the floorboards with each angry step. "Where's the fucking talent, Zeke? Huh? You promised me some fresh girls, and it's time you delivered." Zeke was still half-asleep, passed out on his stomach, with his arm nestled between someone's soft breasts. Aunty Mabel ripped the sheets off of Zeke and slapped his bare ass. "You're costing more than you bring in, and I can toss you out at any moment," she said, pointing her long index finger at him. Then she pointed that same finger at the girl. "And you," she said.

"Yes, Mama Mabel," the girl said and peeled Zeke off of her. He didn't remember her name, but she was one of the hefty ones. He liked a woman to have something to grab hold of. She was out of the room faster than he could get himself to sit on the side of the bed, cradling his pounding head in his hand.

"We need some young ones," Auntie said. "This house is supposed to be The Garden Room. A room of fresh flowers. Not the Funeral Parlor. Do what you need to do, or you can get out. I don't care if you're my blood." She bent over and squeezed his face the way she did when he was a boy. "Everyone can be replaced, Zeke. Everyone. Even family."

She let him go, but he could still feel her fingers on him. Before she left the room, she took a long look at him, from head to toe, and then rested her gaze between his legs. He realized then that he was naked. "And you'd better get that thing looked at," she said. "Unless you want it to fall off."

With that she was out the door in a swish of rose perfume and miles of satin fabric.

Zeke shook his head, but his thoughts didn't clear. It took him a moment to realize that if he didn't get some new talent in here soon, then she really would throw him out. He'd have to get a regular job, and he wouldn't have access to all the soft breasts and wide hips that he loved so much.

He also realized that she was right about getting a doctor to take a look at him, but maybe it could wait until tomorrow. He'd just go back to sleep and he'd get his Auntie some sweet young flowers in the morning. He'd do anything, anything to stay in this beautiful life.

❧16❧

The heat no longer affected Lillian the way it had when they'd first come to Chicago two months earlier. They'd arrived during a summer blast of scorching temperatures that seemed like it would never break, and Lillian was a peeled, boiled egg, tender and pure and white.

Newsboys called out headlines of bodies pulled from apartments where people had actually cooked to death. Lillian had been horrified, had nightmares about those bodies pulled from the roaster, crisp and tender as a slab of ribs. Now she thought, *serves them right for not getting out of the building.* A person was accountable for their own suffering, even their own death. *Take control,* she thought. She wasn't a peeled egg, anymore.

It was another day like all the others, though cooler now, the crisp smell of fall in the air. Mother slept fitfully. Lillian knew the apartment had developed its own funk, a living smell of decay that clung to the walls, the floors, and was seeping into the very pores of their skin. It no longer bothered her. She just woke up in the morning, read a little if it was early, pulled on her stiff dress, and walked to work.

She did not feel or react or suffer, anymore. She was beyond that. Her heart had become leather, wrapped in threads of steel. She could feel her insides still shifting and changing. Her blood was not the same as it had been in Michigan. It was thickening. Coursing through her at a slower pace. Fighting harder to reach her fingers, her toes, her brain. It started the day after the fire. Lillian awoke early—really, she'd never even slept—and she ran to the stockyard to ask about Chester. She found the foreman and she ran up to him, her chest heavy with hope, and cried "Chester! Is he all right? Where is he?"

The foreman looked at her and spat a long stream of brown that arched until landing in a puff on the dirt. "Chester who?" he asked.

"Chester! The boy! He runs for…"

There was something in the foreman's eyes then. A flicker of something. And then it was gone, but Lillian understood. "I don't know what you're talking about, girl. I've never known any Chester. And if you want any work today, you better get to where you're needed."

That was the moment her blood coagulated within her veins. The foreman did not know Chester. There was no Chester. Chester was ash. *He should have known better,* she thought. *He was so smart. So bright. He should've smelled the fire starting and got out. It's his own damn fault.*

So she went to the small room where she sorted and cleaned the eggs. At lunch she walked up to one of the men with the bats and told him she wanted to make more money. "The only other job for a kid like you," he said, "Is with the pigs. It pays more but it's not something for a little girl."

"I'm not so little," she said, raising her chin.

"No. I can see that." And he looked her up and down the way that men sometimes looked at mother. Lillian didn't even flinch. "Those pigs are mean. Just the other day, one of them bit a man. Bit off one of his fingers. Whole."

Still, Lillian didn't flinch. "I've got ten fingers," she said. "I can afford to lose one or two."

The man laughed and clapped her on the shoulder. "Go over there. Tell them Patrick O'Neal says you've got the balls for it."

That day Lillian carried slop to the pigs and chased chickens and helped lead the pigs to the slaughter pen. She flinched at the screaming, but eventually, she got used to it. She ran amongst the piss and the shit and the blood. The feathers and the entrails and the racks of meat, swinging, beginning the swift decomposition in the sun. She fell down and got a gash on her leg, but she made fifty cents. She gave her mother a quarter. "Look, Mother," she said, using the voice she used to have but no longer belonged to her. "I made a quarter today. A whole quarter!"

The other quarter she hid beneath a loose board when Mother fell asleep. It was easy. Mother was always sleeping. And this quarter would, by the day, multiply until Lillian, like a cicada emerging from its fragile shell, could escape this carapace.

So Lillian had changed. Lillian would not be a cooked corpse pulled from a sweltering room.

She woke up early. Before the sun even dawned. She picked up her book and read the page again. There was something soothing to her about the chapter on parasites. There were insects that developed inside the growing bodies of caterpillars, taking over their souls from the inside out. Lillian thought that maybe this was what her mother suffered from. An internal plague of locusts. But there were other parasites, too. "There are other insect enemies which attack them from the outside and devour them bodily." And Lillian knew that this was her, or it would be if she weren't careful. She needed to be tough on the outside as well as on the inside. There were parasites and beetles everywhere.

She closed the book. She put on her dress. She left her mother sleeping on the sunken bed. She walked steadily to work.

Cora moaned. The world was too bright and too hot and too mean. Her ankle still hurt. What she really needed was a little more of that laudanum. Laudanum made the world soft and fluffy as cotton candy.

Her skin was alive and prickly. Someone was knocking on the door. Mr. Andersson. He had a key. He smelled like onions, and he had a key. She heard the door open and someone talking. Two someones. I already paid for the rent, she tried to say, but she couldn't seem to find her voice. She was still sore from paying. She would always be sore from paying. Someone was calling her name. Someone was touching her cheek, and it hurt her. It was like a burn to her skin. Why did everything hurt? Why couldn't she laugh and glide and giggle? The hand grabbed her and for a moment it was her father's hand and her father's breath on her lips, and she tried to shove him away.

"Oh, you don't want me now," the voice said, but it was not her father's voice. No. It was Zeke's. It was Zeke in her bed, leaning over her, touching her cheek. "Wake up, little one," he said. "I've got something for you."

His voice was a song. "You've come back!" she said, and she started to cry, either from the sheer joy of having him in her bed, or from the pain of his return.

"I've come back. I've come to help you out. But you've got to help me, too." He rubbed her cheek, and she began to purr like a kitten. She was a kitten, and he was her cream. "Can you help me, too?" he asked.

"Anything," she said. "Anything you ask!"

"That's right, Cora. That's what old Zeke likes to hear. Let's sit you up. We can have a drink together, me and you, and talk things through."

"You brought me a drink?"

He laughed then, and she liked that she could make him happy. "I brought you a special drink. We'll drink up and then..."

"You'll help me, and I'll help you," Cora finished. She was a schoolgirl, and she'd just answered the test question correctly.

"That's right. You'll help me. And I'll help you."

Cora nodded. Her face hurt from the smile that stretched across it but she didn't care. All was well, now. She had suffered, and she had paid, and now Zeke would make everything okay, again. "Dancing," she said, and it was barely a breath.

"You want to go dancing? I'm not sure you can even walk." She heard him moving around then and the sound of a bottle opening. "But this will make you float."

He'd brought her the special drink. Zeke knew her, and he'd come to help her, and he made everything better. He placed the cup to her lips, and she drank deeply. Before she floated away, she looked at him and focused, intently trying to see him for who he was, and she spoke very slowly and carefully so that he would understand. "Anything. You. Want."

He held her then, and Cora smiled at the magic of it all.

❧❧❧

It was a bad day at the factory, but Lillian didn't want to think about it. She wanted to eat some dinner, stop somewhere, eat a real dinner for once instead of just a hunk of bread, but she knew she couldn't go anywhere outside of the district without people staring at her, holding their nose. Her appearance and stench made her one of the invisible-but-seen. People crossed the street as she approached, but never acknowledged they saw her.

She did not have anything to change into, and scrubbing at the dress did no good, anyway. The scent of slaughtered pigs seeped from her skin. She was alive with it.

She walked to her room. Mother would be waiting, and maybe she could get her to wake up, run down to the pub for them and bring back some food. Her mother did nothing all day, just soaked in her own misery. The least she could do was act like a mother for a half hour and make sure Lillian had some food.

When Lillian reached the door to their room, she felt something was wrong. She heard the buzz of beetle wings flying through the cracked door. It wasn't locked, but gaped open. And there was laughter floating out to the hallway. Her mother's laughter, but not her mother's laughter at the same time. Her mother's voice was high-pitched and fluttery. When Lillian peaked inside, she saw why. Zeke was there, his hand shoved between her mother's legs, rustling the fabric of her dress. Lillian knew she should turn and run. She should be a good girl and not see this. Not know that it existed. Instead, she opened the door. Zeke's hand stilled, but her mother kept giggling.

"Oh, Lillian!" she called, her cheeks feverish looking. "You're home! Look who's here! Zeke!"

Zeke smiled and slowly pulled his hand out from her mother's dress. He shrugged as if to say "What can you do?" He said, "Caught red-handed," and then he and her mother laughed and laughed and laughed.

They were drunk, Lillian knew. Or worse. It would explain her mother's lethargy and the too bright flashing of her eyes. But it wouldn't explain why they'd come here in the first place. That was all her mother's fault.

"I need to go to sleep," Lillian said. "I've got to work in the morning, and I'm tired."

Zeke stood up and walked over to her. "Good God, girl. You reek. What happened to the pretty flower you once were? Two days in the city and you've already spoiled?"

"Two months," she corrected. "And I'm not a piece of fruit. It's just the dress."

"Well, you can't come work for me like that. No no no. No one's going to want you smelling like a sewer." He leaned in, his mouth nearly against her neck, and inhaled deeply. "No. You don't smell like a sewer. You smell like a corpse in a sewer. I'm afraid, Cora, that this changes things. I offered you two hundred, but she's only worth one fifty now. I'm being generous. Other houses wouldn't offer you more than one."

Cora waved her hands and giggled. "Two hundred, one fifty, it doesn't matter," she said. "I trust you, Zeke."

Lillian didn't understand. She thought about what Chester had told her about his sister, and she thought about the cows mounting, and dragonflies fused, and she thought she would be sick. "I won't go anywhere with you," she said, her voice soft but with a bit of steel to it.

"Keep it up, and I'll lower that to one twenty five," he whispered, still leaning close "and your mother will starve before the snow falls."

He reached into his pocket and pulled out a wad of bills. He began to count as he walked over to Cora. "Look, Cora! It's raining!" he said and he rained the bills over her where she clapped and clapped, like an idiot child.

"Money!" she cried.

"Buy yourself something pretty," he said. "You deserve it."

Then he turned to Lillian and grasped her by the arm and Lillian froze, the way prey will freeze when trapped in its predator's teeth. It's the last thing they do before they die.

"Come on your own, or I'll just take you."

Lillian didn't answer. She couldn't. She was frozen. She was about to die. Zeke looked her over again and nodded, as if he'd decided something. Then he took out a handkerchief from his back pocket and held it to her nose, covering her mouth too. "I'll take you, then, little one. You're mine now, fair and square."

The last thing Lillian heard before the world fell black, was the sound of her mother laughing, laughing, laughing into the crisp night.

❧17❦

CORA

Oh, the joy! The elation! The love! Zeke loves me and will take care of me, and he is here to help me. I am free from worry and pain. And Lillian…Lillian? Do I feel sorrow for her? I do. I love her. She is my daughter, but it's time for her to pay her own way. A woman can only give away so much of herself before she fades away entirely, and I was so close to fading away.

Every day, I became a little more transparent. I could see the room through my own hand. My feet stopped touching the ground. So I had to let Lillian go. She can make it. I have taught her to be strong, to be fierce. But I have paid enough, and it's her turn now. It is a sacrifice to lose her, but it's time. She's not a little girl, any more. And her need of me is too much. Zeke will take care of her. He will make sure that she is not hurt, not too much, not beyond bearing, and I can have the life I deserve. The life I earned.

One hundred and fifty dollars! This is money for my blood and pain. It is money that will give me a new start. I can buy a new dress, a better one this time. Eat at a good restaurant. One with linen. I can get creams for my hands and make them young again. Zeke will look at me with love, and he and I will marry, and all of this, my life until this point, will have become a trial…a story that I have suffered through to earn my reward.

A woman cannot make it on her own in this life. She needs a strong man to take care of her. John was weak. My father was weak. But Zeke is strong. He is a real man, and he loves me.

He loves me, he loves me, he loves me.

Isn't this money proof of that? Isn't this love? Love bubbles within my chest. It escapes from my throat as laughter. It lifts me, and I dance in the shabby room. I dance and twirl. My ankle is not swollen, and it does not hurt because I am free of John and the effort of being a mother, and I am young again with the love of a strong man. This money, these one hundred and fifty pieces of paper will buy me everything I have ever needed. It has been such a long road. Such a trial. But I have finally succeeded. I finally have what has been coming to me all these long, hard years.

☙18☙

She could smell apple blossoms. Apple blossoms and peaches, and Lillian licked her lips. "Oh, look!" a voice said. "She thinks she's a cat. Look at her little pink tongue." There was a lyrical swing to the voice, and Lillian liked it.

"She's not a cat. She's a pussy. Here pussy, pussy." This voice was harsh and followed by laughter. Lillian's head hurt, and the lovely scent of fruit blooming shifted to the cloying death smell of lilies. She hated lilies. They covered the dead with lilies to hide that the body rots. The body is organic, and that's something no one likes to know except for scientists.

"She's cute. She's wee, isn't she? She can't be ten years old, can she? Is that legal?" The swinging voice.

The harsh voice: "Legal? The only thing in this town that ain't legal is happiness. If you're happy, you're dead. She's plenty legal, or she will be once Mama Mabel gets through with her."

"Sit up, wee one," the other said, and Lillian felt soft pats on her back and someone trying to help her. Everything hurt. Even her eyelashes. "It's all right. You're all right."

"Don't lie to her. She's not all right. She's never going to be all right, again."

"Rachel! That's enough from you! Leave her alone."

The girls around Lillian began to take shape. They were in their undergarments, but they were like no undergarments Lillian had ever seen. She was surrounded by them, these girls. Or were they women? They looked made up like women, but you could tell that underneath the makeup they were young. Maybe as young as she was. Except Rachel seemed older. She had wild brown hair, piled high on her head. She wore a bustier and her breasts were so large, they were nearly pushed to her chin. Her skirt was multicolored and slightly see-through. She could not see the girl holding her, but she could feel her soft breath on the back of her neck. "You call me by my real name again, Buttons, and I'll knock your block off. There's no Rachel here. Not anymore. Not ever, again."

The girl holding her, Buttons, squeezed her shoulder. "I'm sorry, Rosie, I didn't mean to. But you remember this, don't you? Weren't you the scaredest when you woke up? We could make it easier for her."

"No one made it easier for me," Rachel/Rosie said and then huffed, turned, and left the room.

Lillian tried to speak. It was like trying to walk after a bad fall, and her voice was weak and wobbly. "What's happened?" she asked, but then she remembered. She saw her mother dancing and twirling and laughing, felt Zeke holding onto her and… Lillian began to buck, pushing the girl off her.

Buttons released her. Lillian shot to her feet and spun around to face her. Any anger she'd felt pulsing through her evaporated. Buttons was just a girl. A girl with fiery red hair, cut to her shoulders and curly. Her cheeks were red, and her eyes a bright green. "I'll warn ya, lass. There'll be lots of people here that can hurt you, but I'll never be one of them. You and me, we're the same. And we're stuck here until we earn our way out." Lillian tried to process her words while figuring out why her voice was so musical.

"You're not from here?" she managed to ask. Of all the questions she could ask, this one seemed the most ridiculous, but it was the one she most wanted to know.

"You've got a good ear, don't you? I'm from Ireland, and then New York, and then Detroit, and then Chicago. My da gave me up in Detroit. I had to ride the train with Zeke, and I don't know which was would be worse. Having to be conscious with that *idgit* for days on end, or to have him knock you out and wake up and already be here. I think maybe you lucked out on that one."

Lillian didn't feel lucky. Her father was dead, Chester was gone, and her mother had sold her for a hundred and fifty dollars. She didn't know what was going to happen to her next, but she was sure that whatever it was, it wouldn't be lucky.

Lillian looked around the room. It was about the size of the room she'd rented with her mother, but a world different. There was striped wallpaper on the walls in alternating colors of rose and ivory. There were vases of flowers in every corner. A large bed covered in shimmery fabric was up against the wall. It would've been beautiful if not for the pictures of women on the walls. The pictures were all around them and it showed women naked, sprawling on furniture, on the ground, their legs parted. Lillian closed her eyes.

"Do you know where you are?" Buttons asked. "If you don't, I'll tell you. It's better that you know. It'll help if we tell you what's going to happen. Maybe then you'll get through it."

Lillian knew what this place was. And she knew what she was here for. She was here because men did things to women, and they were going to do them to her. "Tell me," she whispered. She couldn't speak too loud. It took all her energy to just say those two words. She didn't want to know, but she trusted Buttons, already. She really had no choice.

And then Buttons told her.

⁂

It was hard to listen to the Schultzes tell him about his wife and daughter and what little they knew of them. It was late at night, and John sat with the Schultzes in their cramped kitchen, talking over the empty plates that had held their dinners and been quickly devoured. Mrs. Schultz, Magdalena, or Magda, as she insisted he call her, sat with her babe at her breast, unashamed of showing her large breast and the dark nipple on which the infant greedily suckled. Magda tended the rooms, cooked, handled billing and dealing with the tenants. Mr. Schultz, Willem, drove their carriage for hire, but also convinced guests to come here and rent, sometimes misunderstanding their directions and taking them here instead of to a requested hotel. "I pull up and show them the good home and good food and they thank me. Well, most do," he said with a smile in his voice. "Others, not so much. But what can you do? Is America, no? Land of the take-what-you-can."

John nodded. The cabbage and sausage sat heavy in his stomach. He hadn't wanted to eat, at all. It didn't seem right, somehow, to sit and eat with these kind people, while his family could be anywhere and was probably suffering. John might have been raised in a small farming community, but he'd travelled enough to know the dangers of the city. Especially for women. Still, he'd eaten. Magda had forced it on him. "If you no eat, how can look for them?" she'd asked, her English good but missing a word or two. Indeed. If he didn't eat, he wouldn't have the energy to go on. He barely had the energy, now, but something pulled at him, a force maybe. Sometimes, he thought he heard Lillian crying for him, but maybe that was wishful thinking. If she was crying, it meant she was alive.

"What we know is not much," Willem said. He nodded and Magda refilled his stein with warm beer, somehow managing this without having the baby unlatch from her breast. She held the beer up to John but he shook his head, a single no thank-you. "Your woman, your Cora, she come her with the girl and want a place to stay that is not too pricey, *ja*, not too fancy. I take them here. They wear clothes that are…" he paused, trying to pluck the right word from the air "…shabby," he said and nodded as if that were just the perfect word.

John's face flushed with heat. Their clothes were shabby. To an outsider, to a German immigrant, his Cora and Lillian appeared poor and uncared for, and whose fault was this? How long had he focused on saving money to the point of ignoring them? He had not tended to them. He had loved Cora in the wrong way.

Willem continued. "She come here, I drop her off, then I go to do my work and do not see them for a week."

Magda picked the story up from there. "Your wife is not so nice." Willem gave her a look. "I must tell him, Willem. If I do not tell truth, he will not know. And the wife was not so nice. She was…her face in the clouds. She laughed too sharp, *ja*? Too happy. There was something not to right. One day she goes out. She is gone all the day. Your girl, Lillian, she stay inside. She hungry. She help me with the guests. She clean and watch the children. She read a book to them about…" Magda said a word in German to Willem.

"Bugs," Willem said, and John's heart clenched. It was the book he'd given her just before he'd left them. They'd left everything, but somehow she'd managed to bring that. Clever girl, he thought. My clever, lovely girl.

"Bugs," Magda agreed. "Lillian is good. Good girl. Then your wife come back, but she is different. She is painted. She is like…like actress on stage. She is not wearing shab-be dress," she paused to look at Willem, proud of picking up his word. "She is wearing bright green dress with stripes the color of…" she seemed to struggle here. She laughed and placed two fingers by her baby's mouth to break the seal on her nipple and out it popped, wet and engorged. John tried not to look, but it was too late. "This color," she said, pointing to the nipple. It was a deep apricot color next to her white skin. She tucked her breast back in her dress, and lifted the baby to her shoulder to try to burp him. John remembered holding Lillian this way, but Cora had never been as carefree with her feeding. She'd seem to resent it, somehow. Magda did it as easily and without shame as she breathed.

"Apricot." John offered. "A green and apricot dress."

"Not good," Magda said and shook her head. "But your Cora act, she act as if she is Queen of England."

"Then she comes to me," Willem picked the story back up. "She ask for work, but not for her. For girl. She wants to know where girl can get work. So I tell them to go to factories. There is lots of work there for the poor. But it is not good work. Lillian goes to work and Cora stays here. Upstairs and…" Here Willem paused. Again, he shared a look with his wife and they seemed to agree.

"Please," John said gently. "You have been so kind to me with telling me this, but I must know everything. If I have any chance…I've got to know it all."

"There was a man," Willem began.

"We do not run that type of house! This is not that kind of place!" Magda said with heat.

"I tell your wife this, and then the next day they are gone. They left owing money. Not much, but enough. I do not know where they went."

So. There it was. John had the truth now, and it was brittle and sharp like a shard of glass. Hold it the wrong way, and it would slice.

The baby burped, and Magda passed the child to Willem who cradled the tiny child in his beefy arms. Then Magda did something that surprised John, so much so that he felt tears threaten behind his eyes before he had a chance to latch them down. She reached across the table and took his hands in hers. They were rough hands. The hands of a hard working woman. But still, they were tender. John had not been held tenderly in years. "Your Lillian," Magda said, taking care to enunciate and get the words right. "She is good. And smart. And strong. You will find her. There is no doubt."

John nodded, because he could not speak.

His daughter was good and smart and strong, but time was running out. He could feel it.

❧❧❧❧

Buttons helped bathe her. Mama Mabel had the large men from outdoors carry up pot after pot of steaming water, and they poured it into a giant tub. Mama Mabel stood in the corner, observing and ordering. She crossed her arms over her huge bosom, seeming to push her breasts up further, almost into her painted face. Lillian thought of a red-breasted robin, heavy with an egg. Maybe Mama Mabel was hatching something.

"You'll only get this treatment once," she said. Lillian tried not to look at her, not directly into her eyes. When you looked into a predator's eyes, they took it as an invitation to attack. Lillian, instead, stared at Mama Mabel's red, red lips and watched them stretch and flap with her words, exposing yellow teeth with each syllable. "For one, you stink to high heaven. I don't think I've smelled worse, even from that girl who had maggots in her twat. You...you smell like a corpse."

Lillian couldn't smell it. Everyone at the slaughterhouse smelled the same. They smelled of death. It was how it was.

"Come on, now," Buttons said, offering her slim hand. "Lift your arms and we'll peel it off you." It was like being peeled, Lillian thought. In fact, some of the clothes were so crusted that Buttons ended up cutting right up the back of her sheath and then tugging until the dress separated from her skin. "Now, in the water. It'll be hot, but we've got to get you good and clean."

Lillian didn't know if she said that for her benefit, or for Mama Mabel and her red, red lips and red hair and red face. There was anger in that woman; Lillian could feel it. She thought of the men with bats in their hands at the factory, of how they watched and would hit the bat against the fat of their palms in silent warning. *Do what I say, or I'll hit you*, their bats had said. Mama Mabel's red lips said the same thing. But even if Lillian did what she was told, Lillian knew she would be hurt, anyway.

The water burned. She was a lobster being cooked. She started to cry and Buttons took up a horsehair brush and started to scrub at her. "Put away the tears," she whispered in her ear. "You've got to be strong now, if you want to get through this. And I want you to get through this. We can be good friends, I just know it. And I need a good friend, too."

Buttons scrubbed. Lillian tried to suck back the tears, but they came, anyway. They mixed with the steam of the water and dropped around her, blending into the bath. When she emerged from the bath, scrubbed red and raw, Mama Mabel made her turn around and around. She lifted her arms and checked her over, looked in her hair, searching for nits, and then told her to sit and spread her legs.

Lillian wasn't sure what Mama Mabel saw there, but it made those red lips smile. Lillian wanted to be sick.

"Tomorrow night, you'll lose that," Mama Mabel said. "And I'll get a pretty penny for it too. My little Zeke did good with you." She laughed then, but it was a sound without mirth. It was a sound that squiggled across the room and burrowed under Lillian's skin where it began to writhe and nibble at her. It was a laugh that just might make her go crazy.

She didn't know what she would lose tomorrow. She thought she'd already lost everything.

❧❧❧

The girl was intact, and Mabel was glad about that one small thing. One, small thing that Zeke had finally managed to do right. That man—that boy really. He'd never grown up—had cost Mabel a pretty penny over the years, and it was about time he started to earn his keep. She'd even contemplated forcing him on his knees to earn a little money. There were men who would pay plenty for the pleasure of taking him, but she just couldn't seem to do that to him. He was, after all, as close to a son as she would ever have. Her sister's boy, who when she looked at him, sometimes made her feel like she was looking straight into her sister's eyes. An eerie thing since her sister was dead and buried two decades ago. Whenever Zeke looked at her, especially when he pleaded with her "No, Auntie Mabel! I can do this! Just give me one more chance!" she saw her sister's eyes in the moment before her death. It was her eyes that had haunted Mabel the most. They'd known. That split second before. They'd known.

That was the last day Mabel earned money the 'decent' way. That night, she'd cleaned herself up and went down to the pub. She charged a dollar per fuck, and she had more money in one night than she and her sister had made their entire time at the factory. That was how the world worked. The good and decent got chewed up and spit out into bits. The tough ones, the lousy ones, the mean ones, they were the ones who survived and prospered. Like Mabel. She'd made a killing over the years. It had only cost her her soul. A soul was overrated, she thought. A soul was nothing but air.

This girl, this body, would make her some real money. For a young one like this, for a girl who was whole and pure, Mabel could get some twisted character to pay fifty or more dollars just for the honor of introducing her to the way of the world. She could turn that fifty dollars into two hundred or more if she made a party of it. She'd earn back what the girl cost her in a single night, and then she'd keep earning for every man that girl brought to her. Mabel would teach her the way. Men were as pliable as mud, even when they were hard as a rock. You just needed to know the right way to handle them to make the coin flow from their pockets.

There was a risk, sure. There were violent men. Men who drank too much. Men who wanted to be in control in the bedroom because they had no control anywhere else in their lives. But this was reality. Reality was hard. It was hard for a woman, but harder still for a girl. She felt no guilt for this Lillian's fate. The girl would either toughen up, or Mabel would wipe bits of her off her sleeves and move on. That was how it worked. You moved on.

But you never forgot the eyes. Those…they stayed with you. Watching.

❦19❧

Cora awoke to a new day. Of course, it was a new day. An old night was followed by a new day. That was how it worked. But it was such a glorious new day. A new day that demanded her attention, her participation, her revelry. Cora threw open the curtains in her flat. The sunlight struggled to get through the filthy windows, but even that didn't bring her down. There was a nice orange-ish hue to it. A nice golden light cast over the dirty floor and her room. The color landed on her cheeks and made her skin seem flushed and young, again. And maybe she was. She felt young, again. She felt as light as a bubble. She had one hundred and fifty dollars and something even more precious: she had freedom. Today, she could do whatever she wanted. Her father was not there, anymore. Hadn't been for years. Her baby brother had long since grown. Who knew where John was, the old sap. And Lillian, her child, had flown the coop.

What would Cora do today? She could eat at a nice restaurant. A restaurant with white linen. A restaurant that served filet mignon and asparagus and chilled wine. She could catch the eye of a handsome stranger, and he would fall in love with her on the spot. "Please," he would say, "may I join you for this fancy dinner?" and she would say "But of course," and he would pay her bill so that she didn't have to dip into her nest egg, and then he would romance her until he married her under the setting sun, and everyone would wear white and applaud her beauty and good fortune.

But first, she'd have to clean herself up. Get out of this God-awful dress and find a place that was better suited to her level of refinement. She looked in the mirror. There were circles under her eyes and her hair was threaded with grey. "It must be the light," she said softly, though her voice rang in the empty room. In the light, her skin seemed translucent. She could see the blue veins running under her hands' skin. And when she looked down at her feet, her dainty ankles had somehow thickened and one was a strange purplish color.

It was just the pallor of her room. It cast a din over everything. She needed to get out of here. But first, before the fancy restaurant and before the new clothes, maybe she could find someone who would give her a little of that laudanum. Just to smooth out the edges. Just to soften things a bit. It had been such a long time since she'd been alone that she suddenly felt unsure of herself. And a sip of that laudanum would be just the thing.

❧❧❧

Chicago was waking up. It seemed to light from within, shadows slowly warming and glowing, then disappearing altogether. John had been awake all night, and this would be the new rhythm to his days. He and Willem had come to an agreement. "Look," Willem said, his voice thick from so much beer, "we can help each other. I will get few new horses. You will drive my carriage at night and look for your family while you take customers around the city. In exchange, we give you room."

"And food," Magda added. "Good room and good food."

"And maybe you keep some of the profit. But not much. Is America, yes? I will be big boss man, and this will help my family, too. I can sleep at night this way."

Magda had laughed. "Sleep," she said as if she hardly believed it. "You will want to practice making more babies. With this one, it's always practice, practice, practice."

Willem had laughed, its richness pouring warm and heavy from his substantial belly. "Who needs practice to make babies? I'm very good at it! But I will take you every chance I get."

He'd pulled Magda onto his lap and kissed her then, and John had turned his head but not before noticing how Magda seemed to melt into her husband, how she seemed to want to be there. Kissing Cora hadn't been like that. Kissing Cora had been like trying to kiss a slab of wood. How had he not known? He'd thought women were just like that: stiff and solid and impossible to make love you. He hadn't known they could be any other way. Maybe his father had been right after all. Cora was a woman who would always be wanting something more. Something more than John.

He had agreed to Willem's offer. Of course he had. It was a better offer than he could have envisioned. He thought he'd work at the docks or on ships, catching and butchering fish. But that would take him away from his search for days, even weeks, at a time. This way, he could explore every street and alley, relying on the power and energy of the horses. He could search. And eventually, he would find them.

After his first night, Chicago was still a mystery to him, and he had no better idea of where to search for them. But his eyes were open, and the shadows were lifting.

When the streets had passed from blue to grey to gold, he pulled up to the Schultz's home. He would feed and water the horses, and then Willem would take over the carriage for the day. John knew he needed to sleep, but he wanted to keep looking. In his room, he lay on the small cot and closed his eyes. In his sleep, he traced the roads, looking for clues to where they had run. Over and over, he went through the streets, certain he had found something. The poor section of town called to him. It went beyond the obvious that Cora didn't have much money. There was something about that section of town...the stench maybe, the sadness, the poverty...that he knew Cora could get lost there. It was a type of living she'd been familiar with, and didn't one always return to the known?

※※※

In Traverse City, Lillian slept in her own room. Morning light spilled through the window and draped across her like a band of fairy gold. In the distance, she could hear a cow mooing. The wind rustled the trees, as if a giant was shaking her hair. Birds sang, and cicadas buzzed. It was musical.

Here, in Chicago, there was music, too, but it was different. It was the music of the underworld, as if Lillian's life had flipped and she went from living a golden life to toiling in the heat of hell. Outside, she could hear the train and carriages. Horses. She could hear an occasional woman's cry. Muffled laughter. She tried not to hear things, but you couldn't close your ears the way you could close your eyes. She'd been awake for hours, maybe, but pretended to sleep.

She was curled up like a potato bug in the corner in a drab room with five other girls. There were two beds and a cot, but Lillian had chosen the corner last night. The walls up against her made her feel penned in and solid, as if she was being held up. She shut her eyes, and she refused to open them. If she didn't open them, she wouldn't have to know that she was here, in this house, instead of in Traverse City with the cool, refreshing bay just a short walk away. Something poked her and she jerked. "She'll never make it." It was Rosie poking her with her foot. Rosie speaking. She didn't even have to open her eyes to know.

"She will," Buttons insisted. Lillian felt Buttons' soft hand on her shoulder shaking her. "Wake up," she said. "Wake up, or Mama Mabel will wake you, and you don't want that."

Lillian opened her eyes. "What do I do now?" she asked. It was the only thing she could think of. Just two days ago, she would have walked to the factory yard and polished eggs and fed the pigs. Before that, she'd have gone to school. But here, where girls lounged around half-dressed, she didn't know what was expected of her. Did she cook? Clean? Could she run away?

"Mama Mabel wants you to get dressed. You'll work for a bit and then…" Buttons' green eyes were sad.

"And then you'll go with Zeke," Rosie finished. Her face was smug. Her hair was still disheveled and she wore a shift so thin that Lillian could see right through it to her bare skin. "And once it's all over, maybe then Buttons can stop moping around so much."

"I'm not moping," Buttons said. "I just…I hate this part. And what are you? Ten? Eleven? Even I was thirteen when I started. It doesn't seem right."

Lillian still didn't want to know what they were talking about, but she had an idea. "Where are my clothes?" she asked. Buttons had told her to get dressed, and that was a tangible thing. That was something she could do.

"Lulu?" Buttons called, and a beefy girl with pigtails handed her a package wrapped in brown paper and tied with a string. "Mama Mabel wants you to wear this."

Lillian took the package, and with trembling fingers unwrapped it. Inside was a navy blue dress with a white pinafore. It was free of stains and looked brand new. Her cheeks flushed as images of a schoolhouse and books and chalk dust filled her mind. "Am I going to school?" she asked, her voice breathy with hope, because maybe this was possible. Good things still happened. Maybe she'd just been confused. But then Buttons looked at her with those sad, green eyes, and she knew. She just knew.

"Mama Mabel wants you to wear this for...tonight."

Rosie laughed. A short laugh. without humor. "You're a lucky one, ain't ya? Most girls come in and Zeke takes care of them right away, but the special ones...oh, the *special* ones get *special* treatment."

Buttons turned on her. "Get out!" she cried, and Lillian jumped. The sudden violence scared her. Buttons seemed to be eternally gentle, but there was steel in there, somewhere. Maybe even a sharp knife-edge. "I'm trying to help her! Can't we for once..." And then she was crying.

Rosie pushed Buttons out of the way. She pulled Lillian to her feet, and Lillian dropped the dress and pinafore. "Look. They want you young and innocent and whole. They'll take you in a room. Zeke will be there, and he'll have a group of dirty old men, and they will hurt you. They will hurt you, so you better suck it up, and be ready for it." She shoved Lillian then and stalked out of the room, the other girls parting to make way for her.

Lillian looked at Buttons, but Buttons would no longer hold her gaze. "You'll get through it. If you think of something else. If you concentrate on that something else. If you just think of that over and over and over, you'll be okay. And if Zeke offers you something to drink, you drink it, okay? Now, get dressed."

Lillian nodded. She wanted to change where there was some privacy, but the other girls just watched her. Their gazes blank and hollow. She thought of the cows in the stockyard and the emptiness in their big, brown eyes. No one else spoke to her. And Buttons had turned away and no longer seemed to know or care that she was there. Lillian put on the crisp navy dress and the starched white pinafore, and though she was clean, she felt dirty.

❧❧❧

Cora tucked her money into her boot for safekeeping. She reserved a coin in her purse, but she knew this area, now, and if anyone noticed her carrying a heavy purse, they'd cut the strings faster than she could blink. She'd get a new place to stay as soon as she could, but she still had a few days on her rent. Oh, how she would laugh when Andersson came to collect his rent. He'd be all puffed up like a rooster, anticipating her bent over the bed, her face pressed into the mattress, him sweating behind her. She would laugh in his face. Spit in his face. Tell him there was another place he could shove his cock. Right into the devil. She'd use those words, too. She was a new person, and she'd use those words like a whip.

For now, though, there were more important errands. Laudanum and food. Maybe a bit of pleasure. Maybe a new dress. The hundred and fifty dollars was warm in her boot and buoyed her. She left her disgusting little room and tiptoed down the hall. She was weightless with hope. Everything would change, now. She'd gone through the trouble of losing John, of having to force Lillian out of the nest so she could fly, and now…now…Cora could do anything.

She felt the smile on her face spread. The smile seeped into her veins. She practically thrummed with it.

It took her only a few blocks to find a drugstore. Funny, how her body was reacting just knowing that she would get a little relief soon from all the drudgery. The heat. The sameness. She hadn't forgiven Zeke yet for all the hurt he'd caused her when he'd promised her so much, but she did thank him for introducing her to this…what would be a good word for it? Elixir. Laudanum wasn't a drug as much as it was an elixir. An enhancer. Something she earned. When she opened the door, a bell chimed, and she entered a small dark room in deep wood, lined with shelves and shelves of bottles. She felt a sort of sexual excitement and wondered if they had anything to enhance that. If she weren't so mad at Zeke right now, she'd let him kiss her wherever he wanted. No. She'd *make* him kiss her wherever she wanted. This was what the new Cora did. New Cora made demands.

"I'd like a bottle of laudanum," she said when the old, hunched man entered the room carrying a box. His hunch, apparently, was permanent. He could not straighten to look at her, but instead tilted his head and looked her up and down. His face was deeply lined, and he had white eyebrows so bushy they boarded on the fantastic.

"Laudanum?" he asked, his voice as brittle as autumn leaves.

"Yes!" she spoke louder this time. "I'd like a bottle of laudanum!"

"What do you want it for?"

Cora paused. Did he need to know? Was it his right? Couldn't she just buy what she wanted since she had the money? How dare he even ask her, treating her like some common misanthrope when she was a lady with a hundred and fifty dollars and about to meet the man who would whisk her away and marry her. Wouldn't this old hunchback feel ridiculous then when he realized she was *somebody*.

But New Cora was hard to give voice to. Harder to give voice to when she realized this little man had the power. Men always had the power, even if they couldn't stand up straight. "I've hurt my foot," she said. She lifted her dress to show him her ankle. It was ringed in purple and blue.

The man was quiet and then gave her a nod. Cora wasn't sure if it was because he got to see her ankle, or because he believed that this was the reason she wanted the drink. "Laudanum cures everything," the man said, almost as if talking to himself. "That's what women seem to think." He turned from her and slouched over to the wall, standing on his tiptoes to reach a small box that held glass bottles in it. Cora was certain he'd drop them, the way his hands shook, but somehow he managed to claw one of the bottles, lift it from the shelf and place it on the counter. He looked at her then, all sideways and hunched over. Any sexual excitement Cora had felt cleared up instantly. His eye looking at her was blue and milky. "It'll cure you of everything if you're not careful. It'll cure you of your very life."

Cora snatched the bottle from him and gave him a dollar and ran from the store. She could hear him laughing all the way down the block as she hobbled back to her room.

❧20❧

What Zeke wanted more than anything was to get this night over with. He wanted to take the three girls he'd lined up, close the doors, wait for the men to do their business, and then he wanted to get back to his room. If he was lucky, Auntie Mabel wouldn't see him come in. He'd leave the money for her in her room, and then he'd slip away. He wouldn't have to deal with her complaints, her abuse, her constant disappointment. "Five hundred dollars? For three young girls? For three virgins? You get a measly five hundred bucks? What's your problem? Maybe I should hire you out instead. Put some rouge on your cheeks, throw you into a room and make you earn some real money." He could already hear her masculine voice, how when she was angry it dropped a decibel, and he could feel it rumble in his chest.

He could never make Auntie Mabel happy.

He would never be good enough, and it was all on account of his mother's eyes. They had the same look, apparently, whatever that meant. After all these years, he still didn't know what had happened between his mother and Auntie Mabel; but whatever it was, it was twisted. And it had killed his mother and forced Auntie Mabel to take care of him.

Tonight, that could all change. He'd tell her he'd made five hundred dollars, but he hoped to double that. The other five hundred would get tucked away into his own stash. Soon, he'd have enough to start his own house, with his own rules, and no one to answer to. If he wanted a girl on her knees for him, he could just snap his fingers, and down she'd go. If he had his own house, the girl wouldn't look at Auntie Mabel for approval, as if she was some kind of God. It wasn't right, the amount of power Auntie Mabel carried. She wrapped herself in it like a mink. Even the mayor answered to Auntie Mabel. The mayor had a particular penchant for young girls and bruising. Auntie Mabel filled his desires and regularly delivered girls to his estate. When Zeke had his own place, he'd get in on that action. He'd weasel his way into the Mayor's good graces, and then take over his business. And who would be weak then?

Zeke looked at himself in the long mirror. He was thin but you could still see the line of muscles beneath his starched shirt, and in the fit of his trousers. His hair was greased back, and his mustache was a delicate line that twirled. Walking down the street, he looked like any other respectable man. That part was key. You had to look respectable. It allowed you to get away with anything, even the darkest kind of pain.

He smiled at his reflection. He had a lot of plans. A lot of goals. And it all started with tonight.

⁊▲⁊▲⁊▲

Lillian had started in the kitchen, washing dishes, but when Mama Mabel found out, she yelled at Miss Eddie, the grey haired woman who was deaf. She seemed to understand Mama Mabel's red face and her words, even though she couldn't hear the shouting. "This one needs to be fresh, Eddie! Fresh! We can't have her with red hands and cuts. Put her upstairs. Have her lay down for God's sake. She'll do plenty of work, tonight!"

Then Lillian was whisked back upstairs to sit with two other girls, both of whom she was "working" with, tonight. Meredith was tall and blonde and looked sixteen, though she wore her hair in pigtails. The other girl was petite, with deep brown hair and golden skin. "She doesn't talk," Meredith said. "She just chews on her fingernails. Maybe there's something wrong with her."

Lillian looked into the girl's brown eyes. They seemed to flash at her with a deep intelligence. "I'm Lillian," she said. "Who are you?"

The girl looked at her and then nodded. "Helena," she said, but her name was said with a different lilt than Lillian was used to.

"Do you speak English?" Lillian asked, careful to speak slowly and enunciate.

Again, the girl looked at her, focusing on her words. Then her eyes filled with tears, and a torrent of words came out, of which Lillian understood nothing. "I can't," she started. "I'm sorry. I don't understand!"

The words kept coming, Helena's voice rising. Then she wrapped her ragged fingers in her hair and started to yank, pulling out a clump of the beautiful brown hair.

"No!" Lillian cried. "Meredith! Help me. Please!"

Meredith grabbed the girl's arms to get her to stop. and Lillian tried to calm her down, the way you coo to a horse to settle it. "It's okay," she said. "It's okay. We're here together, and we'll be fine. This is a nice house. They'll take care of us."

Helena seemed to calm. Meredith released her arms and breathed a short laugh. "You don't really believe that, do you? You know what they're doing, right? Some men are going to have their way with us tonight, and if we do a good job, maybe, maybe we can stay here and get diddled every night. And maybe if we don't get a baby or a disease or something, we can work off what we owe Mama Mabel, and then maybe we can get out of here. But until then, we're screwed. Literally." Meredith shrugged. She said everything without emotion. No anger. No sadness. Just a calm kind of acceptance.

"We could run," Lillian said. "We'll open the window and we'll…"

Meredith cut her off. "What? Climb down? You see those brutes out there. They'll squash us like a bug. Splat! And then Mama Mabel will kick the tar out of us. No. Some things you just gotta do. My neighbor used to diddle me all the time. At first, it was because I was curious, but then I just couldn't get him off me. If you just let them have at ya, they'll finish in no time, and then you can get on with the rest of your day." Meredith sat on the edge of the bed, popped the end of one of her pigtails into her mouth and sucked.

Helena leaned against her, her breath hot on Lillian's neck.

Lillian did not cry or argue, anymore. She simply sat and waited. And watched as the outside light brightened, burned, and then began to dim. It felt like it took forever, but finally, it began to turn blue outside. The door opened and Zeke stood there. Mother's Zeke. His hair slicked back. His mustache curled. His clothes pressed. He gave them a giant smile and said, "Showtime, girls!"

❧❧❧❧

Cora opened her eyes. It was dark out, and she wasn't sure if that meant that it was morning or night. The lovely woozy feeling had faded, and she was left with a peculiar hollow feeling. She wasn't sure if it was hunger or just the pain of awakening to an empty room. For so long, all she'd wanted was to be left alone. Now, that she was, she felt like she was disappearing, the way that fog slowly dissipates in the morning; one moment it's just…gone.

Yes, shouldn't she be celebrating? She should! She was a free woman, and all of Chicago was at her fingertips. Had she a better view, she'd have thrown open the curtains and called out "Hello!"

But her room looked out on the dirty street. The factories puffing dark smoke in the distance. Tomorrow, she would find a new place to rent. This place was for the lost. The forgotten. The foggy ones.

She climbed out of bed, feeling light, again. Oh, she should have purchased a different dress, but it was dark, and in the moonlight, she would shine. She just needed to do up her hair a bit smoother. Pinch her cheeks for a bit of extra color. If she had a beet, she'd cut it and use it to blot a bit on her lips and cheeks. Emphasize what was there but was only sleeping: her youth.

Tonight, she was alone, and it was glorious. Tonight, she could go anywhere, do anything, be anyone. Tonight, she would be the belle of the ball. She danced around and around in her room, laughing lightly to herself. She stopped abruptly when she noticed the book in the corner. That book about bugs. That book that John bought for Lillian, for their daughter. She felt rage then, a slow boil at her toes. Rage to be reminded that John existed, at all. That even now he breathed out there, his claws reaching out to her to pin her down. That Lillian, who looked so much like a younger Cora, had the whole of life ahead of her.

Lillian did not have wide hips yet or the stretched skin of childbirth. Lillian didn't have to bear the sweaty embrace to pay the rent. Lillian read books on bugs and dreamed of being a scientist. Lillian could be a scientist for all Cora knew, and it angered her. It made her shimmer with rage. Always. There was always someone in Cora's life that was more blessed than she was. Someone that got all the riches. Cora earned that one hundred and fifty dollars she'd been given for Lillian's purchase. She earned that and so much more. One day, she'd collect.

She picked up the book, ran to the window, opened it, letting in the fetid Chicago night air, and tossed it outside.

She'd had enough of bugs in her life. Good riddance to all the things that crawled in the dark.

Cora was going to dance in the light. Cora was going to shine.

❧❧❧

John missed the smell of the bay, the gentle rocking of the boat. He missed the ache in his arms from hauling in lines filled with whitefish. He liked the sound of the knife scraping against a fish's scales. How the scales flecked up like silver snow. But the carriage he drove rocked a bit, bounced on the dirt road, and for now, that was enough. He tried to stay focused. He tried not to think of home. Of Lillian running down the lane to meet him and throwing herself in his arms, oblivious to the smell of fish and muck. He'd always wanted Cora to run and embrace him in that way. Felt that love should be shown and shared. The most he got from her was a peck on the cheek after carefully wiping her hands clean on an apron. He wondered if she carefully wiped her lips when she turned away from him. The truth of her lack of feeling for him, her abhorrence of him, kicked him the gut. It was enough to hollow him out, the way a log sometimes rots from the inside to the out.

He tried not to think of this. Better to focus his mind on the Chicago streets. His starting point was always the same, but where he ended up was an unknown. He'd start at the pier, picking up weary travellers and taking them to all manner of places. He could tell from the type of dress and the amount of luggage if he was going to the north side of Chicago with the wide and open mansions, or a modest hotel, a cheap room, and sometimes, for the sailors mostly, a brothel. Those who were truly poor did not hire his services, but walked tiredly past, perhaps with a bit of yearning in their eyes. He'd have given them a ride for free if he could, but he needed to earn his keep and keep Willem and Magda happy. The best hope he had of finding his daughter—and Cora—was to get to know the city, intimately.

He took all sorts of fares to do just that. After only a week of working, he was already familiar with the best restaurants in town, the hotels where they greeted you with servants wearing white gloves. He knew where the high-end brothels were, and the red light district where a man could walk by open doorways and look at a collection of women who showed all they offered if you had a bit of coin. Was he tempted by their soft shapes, the flare of a hip, the dark hair visible even in the shadows? Tempted. Yes. It would be nice to lose himself for a while. To feel the full potential of his body with another. But the thought that, maybe like Cora, the woman hated the feel of him, his scent, his touch, it made him wither. There would be plenty of time for loving once he got his world in order. Once Lillian was home and they were settled. Once he'd seen Cora and maybe let her go.

He didn't have the energy, anyway. He flicked the reigns to get the horses moving, and the carriage jerked. The man and woman in back huddled close together, the man's hand buried in the woman's dress. The woman who was not his wife, but someone he clearly knew intimately. John was taking them to The Blackstone Hotel, a fancier place, and the man who'd hired him gave him a look that told him not to ask any questions. John wouldn't ask. And maybe he would be rewarded with a generous tip.

The carriage rocked. The woman behind him sighed softly, the sound light and warm. The night, for once, was cool. The relentless heat had broken for a bit, and a breeze blew in off the lake. There was a slight hint of fish in the air, and John inhaled deeply. It calmed him. He was lulled by the passing streets, the rattle of an occasional streetcar. The buzz of gaslights being lit by men with long poles. Chicago at night, was a different city. It was bathed in a sort of magic, filled with both the possibility of wonder and horror. John's eyes were heavy. Sleep called to him. He was not fully used to switching to working nights, and sometimes the weight of wanting to sleep pushed on his shoulders. The rocking of the carriage lulled him.

Restaurants were full, and women and men walked the streets in their finery. Off to the theater, maybe. To walk the promenade. To hear a concert. He saw a small group of school children walking. Maybe three or four, along with two adults dressed in crisp linen suits. He wondered where they were going at a time like this. They were schoolgirls, and his eyes blurred with the sudden rush of tears. He did not cry, but the tears stayed with him, even as he turned the corner, and the horses plodded steadily on and on, deeper into the coming night.

૪ટ&ટ&

The boy had been waiting for days, huddled in the shadows. He begged for money when he could. He'd have used what little was given to him to buy food, but it hurt to eat. Of course it hurt to eat. His mouth would never be the same. After the fire, they'd held him down, and though he'd promised, he'd promised he would never ever tell, they still cut out his tongue. Maybe he should've died. But Chester was like a cat with nine lives, though he figured he was at least on his tenth or eleventh, by now. He had nowhere to go, so he went the only place he could think of. He went to find that girl, the one who reminded him of his sister Meg. That girl. What was her name? He'd called her Cherry, hadn't he?

In his mind, Cherry was changing and morphing into Meg. And Meg would gather him in her arms, wash and tend his wounds, and heal him with her love. It was the only thing he had left to believe in.

He stood looking up at her window when suddenly it opened and something plummeted to the ground. The pages flapped and fluttered like it was some bird that was trying desperately to take flight. It landed with a thud and a puff of dirt. Chester poked it with his foot to make sure it was dead. Of course it was dead. Books were never alive to begin with, and that's what it was. A stupid old book. Only…this book…this book was hers. He'd seen her reading it when he'd followed her. He flipped through the pages. He couldn't read a word of it but there were pictures. Real live pictures of butterflies and caterpillars. They were gross and wonderful. Tucked in the pages was a postcard. It was bent and fading, but Chester could still make out the light hue of pink blossoms, the green green hills. It was a cherry orchard, with a lake stretching out from side to side across the postcard. A cherry orchard.

This was her postcard, and her book. He looked up at the window and felt like he was looking up at heaven. He couldn't read this book, but he'd learn. They might've taken his tongue, but he still had his hands and his brain and his spirit. And Chester was a very smart and resourceful boy. He'd find the girl again, and she would make everything better.

೮⧠೮⧠೮

Cora was aglow. She had never felt so light. She danced out of her room and out of the boarding house. Not even the sight of a grubby little street urchin with his nose in a book could bring her down. She walked two blocks and then waved for a cab. She was loaded now; the money in her boot was hot and sent a lovely buzz through her veins. She would take a cab to the good part of town.

A man pulled over. He was handsome. "Where's a beautiful young thing like you off to?" He was American, thank God, and smiled an adorable gap toothed smile. He was blonde with a bush mustache and Cora wondered what it would be like to kiss him.

"I'm off to a dinner. A nice dinner, I think."

"On your own?"

"Well," she faltered. Wondered if he disapproved. "I'm new in town and I don't really know anyone. I had family but...my grandmother...the poor dear." Magically, tears filled her eyes. Cora made her lip tremble.

"Ah. You poor dear. A woman like you…on her own in Chicago? Why, that's a travesty! Tell you what, why don't you sit next to me here and we can make a night of it? Me and you."

He smile was as bright as the moon.

Finally. Finally a man treated her with some respect. Cora noted his white suit and white shoes. His shirt was stiff and starched. This was a man with a significant income who could take the night off from work and show her the town.

"What a lovely offer," she said, blushing. She offered him her hand and he helped her into the cab.

⁂

Zeke had the three girls drink something and then, along with Franz—the outside guard—put them in a carriage. Lillian felt woozy. The world began to blur. Next to her, Helena clutched her arm and burrowed in as close as she could get. Meredith held her hand out in front of her and said "pretty". It was just one night, a few hours at most, Buttons had told her. "You'll be fine," she assured the girls, looking at Lillian and holding her gaze. "Just keep your mind on something else."

"And take whatever they give you," Rosie offered. She was watching the girls get ready.

Buttons glared at Rosie. "I mean," she amended. "Take the drugs. Zeke's going to offer it to you. Take it."

And Lillian had. She didn't want to disappoint Buttons. She wanted to be strong. But most of all, she wanted to make it through this alive. In her book, she'd read of insects falling upon a host and consuming it whole. She was afraid that was what was going to happen to her.

They rode for what felt like forever, the carriage rocking her back and forth. The streets went from piss-smelling to green grass along the curb. The buildings changed from brick houses squeezed together, to sprawling white mansions and gleaming church spires. "We'll get out, here," Zeke said, and the carriage pulled over. Lillian and Helena huddled together. It was hard to walk, and everything was so blurry. She felt someone grab her to steady her, but she wasn't sure who or why.

A carriage drove past them, and in her haze and growing delirium, Lillian thought she saw Papa. It was enough to make her heart seize up inside her. She looked at her feet and concentrated on putting one in front of the other.

Zeke had booked the floor of a hotel. They walked in to a party filled with men in black suits and top hats, drinking and laughing. When the three girls entered, the men turned as one, a flock of predators. A murder of crows. Helena was forced out of Lillian's arms, and Lillian stood in the room, surrounded but alone at the same time. She thought she heard Meredith laughing and calling someone a 'dirty old prick'. She thought she heard crying. She couldn't be sure.

Then someone grabbed her hand. He was tall and old. She had to look up to see him. She saw the bottom of his chin, a flash of yellow teeth. "Come here, little one. Aren't you a peach? Aren't you just lovely? Come see your daddy. I've got something to teach you."

Daddy? She thought. Didn't they mean Papa? Was papa here?

She was lead into a room and then...

Lillian focused on other things. She clung to thoughts from long ago. She tried to survive the night and the grubby, desperate, and scratching paws against her flesh.

❧21❦

LILLIAN

My name is Lillian March. Lillian Annabel March. And I live in Chicago, but this is not my home, oh no. This is just a place. I live in Traverse City, Michigan. By the bay and the cherry orchards. My name is Lillian Annabel March, and...I can see the bay from my house. It is blue and green and sometimes in the wind you can smell fish. You can smell fall. You can smell snow. But not today...today...oh god...My name is Lillian March and I am eleven. I am twelve. Didn't I have a birthday? I did. I had a birthday, and Mama made me a cake and Papa, oh, Papa was there, and it is my birthday, and I am twelve years old. I am ten years old. I am six years old. My name is Lillian. And. And. And. There is a cherry orchard, and I sit there, and I read, and I read, and I am a scientist. I will be a scientist, and I will study insects and the lives and...something is different. There is pain. But it is okay. I am only changing. My bones are cracking. Oh god. They crack and snap, but I can get through this because after they have broken they will re-fuse. They will be at different angles. My bones will be stronger and...My name is Lillian,

Lillian, Lillian. When will this stop? Who could do this? Who would let them do this? Zeke. Zeke, I hate you. You are evil. And Mama. You did this. You did this more than Zeke. You are no mother, no mother, no mother. No mother to allow…I live in Traverse City. There are cherries. The world is white. I. My. I. Lillian. I am Lillian, and I…can't…feel. Anything. My bones have broken. My skin is weeping blood. I will not survive this. I will not. I will. The cherries are in bloom, and the world is white, but I am red, and there is something burning, burning, burning, and my bones have re-fused and my muscles are strengthening, and if I get through this, I will make everyone pay for this. I will make them pay. My name. My name. I am Cherry. Lillian is no more. Lillian is dead.

PART THREE
FALL

1910

CHICAGO

❧22❧

The secret to running a successful whorehouse, Mabel knew, was that you didn't call it a whorehouse. As soon as you referred to the women as whores, men would shit all over them. Sometimes, literally. And she wanted her girls to be taken care of. The things they did, they deserved to be worshipped. Life was hard and ugly and bloody. The least that she could do was give them a soft place to lie down, medical attention when needed, and to cover the reality of what they did with a gauzy sheen. Make the world sparkle. That's why she called her house The Garden Room. Each room, a different kind of flower to be plucked. Each girl a different beauty in a bouquet. Or some such malarkey.

She did not run a whorehouse. She ran a house of pleasure. A boudoir. They threw parties where men were adored. Where they were made to believe they were irresistible. It wasn't their beauty or power that made them irresistible. Certainly not the power of their cocks. They were irresistible because of the money they offered. Once that money was gone, Mabel could care less about them. But she did care about the girls. She cared about them, but when they were used up, they were tossed out, too. This was real life, honey. Get used to it, or get out.

She'd made some poor decisions over the last two decades. Decisions that haunted her at night. That night with her sister, for one. But maybe that was because it had been her first bad decision. It wasn't to be her last. She'd made plenty of mistakes. That girl, just a few months ago. Mabel had known she was fragile. Mabel could tell it just by looking at her. That girl, whoever she was, didn't make it, and she'd had to have Zeke take her little body to be put to rest. That was a bad decision. It cost money and time and it made Zeke all moody and difficult. And Mabel had made other decisions over the years. Decisions that cost her money and time and maybe a bit of her soul. Every year she had a little less to give. There were decisions she'd made that had almost caused *her* to be put to rest. She'd ended up battered and black and blue and near death more than once. But she'd learned from her mistakes. A woman with a house, with a business, had power. And this was hers. The Garden Room and all her flowers. It sounded so pretty, didn't it?

She'd just made some decisions this morning, and while it pained her, she wouldn't let it show. Nothing ruined a well-oiled business more than sentiment. Rosie was used up. She'd always had an attitude problem. Later, she'd been drunk most of the time with a bad attitude. Now, she was taking drugs. Mabel wasn't sure what exactly, but it was something new. Something that people said was good for you. Mabel knew better. Nothing you shot up into your veins would ever be good for you. Ridiculous. So. Rosie. Not even eighteen yet, and she'd be out on the street. If she was lucky, one of the lower houses, an actual whorehouse, would take her in. If she wasn't lucky, and Mabel thought she wouldn't be, they'd pull Rosie's bloated body from the river before Christmas.

It pained Mabel. It did. Right in her heart.

The truth was, Cherry, the youngest of her girls, was something special. It had only been a couple of months, but already she'd earned her fee three times over. She needed to be moved up. Her own room, now, maybe. God knew, the girl had earned it. There was something about her that Mabel's patrons couldn't get enough of. She was sweet, they said. So pure. So innocent. After all the times Cherry had been locked up with a patron, there couldn't be an inch on her body that was actually innocent, but still, she made the men believe.

In this business, making the men believe was akin to magic. And Mabel's house needed a little magic. So Rosie was out. And Cherry....Cherry would get a room all to herself. Mabel hoped she would last. She cared about the girl. Yes, she did. If she could only last. At least a year. A year of that girl's magic would build a nice little nest egg for Mabel. And then, maybe, she could finally get out of this fucking business. Take away the sheen, the fancy bedrooms, the booze. And that's all this place was. A business for fucking.

It was an ugly, ugly world. And that was the goddamned truth.

☙☙☙

Something was wrong with him, Zeke knew. Ever since that night he'd carried that poor dead girl, no more than a doll draped in his arms to toss her into the river...something had happened to him. Something dark and twisted had gotten inside of him. He could feel it slithering right beneath his skin. Like some kind of thin worm with spines. That's what it felt like. He looked at his bare arm. Thought he saw it, maybe. But no. That was just the line of one of his blue veins. He thought he saw it move.

It was that girl. That poor girl, Helena. He'd watched her bob in the water and it was as if he was looking at the ghost of his mother. And maybe he understood then that she had died because of the appetites of men, and he had fed them. He could barely look at the other two girls because of the shame of it. Meredith seemed no worse for wear…but Lillian…or Cherry as she called herself now, Cherry made him want to tear his eyes out.

He tried to shake the thoughts from his head as he lathered the shaving cream with the stiff brush. Round and around in the bowl, then slathered it on his face like he was some kind of cake to be frosted. He couldn't get the thoughts out of his head. How that night he'd had plans to take all the money, and escape. Start his own business. Be his own boss. Stop answering to Auntie Mabel and her huge breasts and doughy thighs and all the things she made him do for her.

He'd find a woman to adore him, the way that Lillian's…Cherry's mother…had looked at him. Like he mattered. Like he meant something.

He sharpened the razor with a few flicks of his wrist, then began the steady and gentle smoothing over his jaw to cut the tiny hairs.

And then that night. The men had been drunk. That was to be expected. But it was what happened when they were all together—they became something new. Some kind of beast. The way they fell on those girls. The things they did. He hadn't realized Helena was in danger until…

He cut himself. A thin streak of blood shot through the white foam. He thought…no. He could've sworn he saw something dark and slimy flick out of the wound. And the wound wasn't a slice, but a circle. A small lesion.

He grabbed a towel and wiped his face clean of the shaving cream. There was a clean strip of hairless chin, the line of red, no lesion at all. He didn't see anything flicking out anymore.

He was making himself crazy.

Zeke needed to clear his head. He could still get out. He could do it, again. One night, and enough money, and he would be free.

He turned to grab the cup and lather more shaving cream, but as soon as he picked it up, his hand began to shake. The cup was heavy.

As heavy as the dead girl had been in his arms when he'd tossed her into the river. He dropped the cup, and it cracked on the floor.

That slithering. He could feel it. It was real. Something was inside him. An evil had entered him that night.

He picked up the razor and shaved the rest of his face without the cream. The razor dragged against his skin, biting him, but it was better to feel that small pain than to think of that girl Helena in his arms and the sad, sad way she'd left this world.

❧❦❧

Buttons and Cherry sat together in the upstairs room, the one with all the cots. This was where they could relax. Where they could take a few moments to forget about tending to men. They could wash themselves. Brush their hair. Rest. But only for a couple of hours—during the dead time of the day. Usually eight to ten in the morning, or so. Those who had spent the night, had stumbled back to their wives, drunk and smelling of sex. And the new ones, the ones that would show up looking to be adored, were at work, or waking up, or shaving in their clean homes, kissing their wives and children, pretending to be respectable.

Cherry looked forward to this quiet time. This dead spell. It was the only time she felt she could breathe. Most of the girls slept. Rosie was still snoring. Her breathing was so loud that Cherry could feel it in her own chest. "There's something wrong with her I think," Cherry said quietly to Buttons who was plaiting her red hair so that the long tresses swirled around the top of her head.

"Nothing wrong with that one. She's as hard as rock. She just sleeps like the dead."

Cherry nodded. Rosie was hard, but she wasn't okay. Cherry could see it in her eyes. She had that same sort of darkness in her that Mother had. Cherry stopped herself there. She had no Mother, now. No real mother would give up her daughter to a place like this.

171

Cherry was an orphan. She had no past and no future. She existed only in the now. "Do you think about it?" she asked. She tried not to, but around Buttons, the words just formed in her mind and slipped out. Buttons was a safe place. A soft bed of sand in an angry lake.

She thought about it before answering. Buttons did that. Buttons thought about the words Cherry said. She took those words in, turned them over in her palm like a shiny stone. She made Cherry feel like what she said mattered. "Do I think about it? You mean my first night here?" Buttons asked.

Cherry nodded.

"It's hard not to, isn't it? The things that happened to you that night. You think how could it possibly get worse. And it does get worse, doesn't it? But somehow, after that first night, you stop feeling it."

"I think I died that night," Cherry whispered, the words so frail they barely had the strength to hold together.

"You did. The old you did. And now, you're a different you. And tomorrow…"

"I'll be different again," Cherry agreed. It was good to be different. It was easier.

"If it hadn't changed you, that night," Buttons said softly, "You'd have ended up like Helena."

They never used the girls' real names. Real names were sacred. But Helena never made it through that night. Helena never had a chance to transform.

"There were only six my first night. You had more, didn't you?" Buttons pinned her hair and reached over to grab Cherry's cold hands in hers.

Cherry didn't answer. She didn't have to. There had been eleven. Twelve if you counted Zeke, though he hadn't done the things to her the others had. But he'd lead them there. He'd poured the drinks. He'd watched. She tried, oh, how she tried not to think about it, or him, or that night. It was such a whirl in her mind, but she still returned to it. She remembered bits and pieces and every now and then a flash would come over her. How one man smelled of peppermint and smoke. How one had a voice like broken glass. How one told her to shush, shush, shush, and then stuffed something in her mouth to shut down her crying.

She remembered because she wanted to. How else would she find them all and kill them? That's what she wanted to do. That night, she'd been Lillian, a girl. But her outer carapace had cracked away, and she'd emerged stronger. Made of blood and metal. Now, she was as fierce as the worst kind of insect. The insects that preyed on others. That laid their eggs in an ant and took over their brains. That grew within another beast and burst out of their bodies and fed on their guts. On the outside, she still looked like a girl. But she wasn't. She wasn't a flower anymore. She was a blood red fruit with a heart of stone.

"We can get out of here someday, you know," Buttons breathed to her. "I've got a plan. I haven't trusted anyone enough to tell them but…oh…you, Cherry. You! I trust you with my life!"

Buttons' eyes were moist with feeling. Though she wanted to feel such passion, too, Cherry couldn't. She was frozen, somehow. "Tell me the plan," she said. What she didn't say, what she just felt instead was, *I need something to believe in.* But maybe Buttons already knew that.

❧❧❧

Chester knew where she was. He'd thought maybe she'd end up back at the factory, and then he'd have lost her for sure. If he showed up at the factory, they'd take more than just his tongue this time. They'd take out his heart, and it'd be pig food. Then he'd be made into sausage. He'd be a boy sausage, and some rich lady would bite into him and eat him all up, and wouldn't that be a story to tell. Course, he'd be dead.

That was the deal.

He promised to keep his mouth shut, they took his tongue, but he got to keep his life. So he would never go back there. But maybe, maybe for Cherry, it would've been better for her at the factory.

He flipped open her book and traced the words he couldn't understand, and then he began to draw. He drew flames that licked around the words, in that white empty space around the corners of each page. Drawing soothed him and he was getting better at it. While he drew, his pencil scratching against the page, he thought about Cherry.

She was in another sort of factory, now, wasn't she? Like his sister, she'd been sold out to stud. Or whatever they called it when the females had to mate against their will. And Chester knew it was against his sister's will, and Cherry's too. And wasn't life just a twisted, dark and painful place? Everyone ended up as a sausage one way or the other.

❧23❧

"**D**on't you think it is time, maybe, to move on? A man like you, you need a woman." Magda was boiling potatoes.

John sat in her kitchen; the potato peels in a pile in front of him. He still wasn't good at it, but he was getting better. He had peeled a bit from his finger.

Magda had laughed and laughed at him, and Willem said, "That is what you get for doing women's work."

It didn't seem like women's work to John. Wasn't work just work? It's what you did to get through the days and nights and months. You needed to work for money, you needed to buy food, you needed to prepare food, and you needed to eat food so you would have enough strength to work. What he didn't need was a woman, though… though sometimes, watching Magda move, her hips round and her bosom buoyant and soft looking, he had to keep his body from reacting. Magda and Willem were his friends. His only friends, it seemed, and he wouldn't let a little desire get in the way of that.

"Of course he should move on. He has moved on! He has moved to Chicago and become a German like us!" Willem's words vibrated in John's chest. "A wealthy German with the money we are making!" He clapped John on the shoulder so hard that John surged forward. "Ach! Sorry, my friend. You are getting weak. That is what the woman's work will do to you."

Magda turned from the boiling potatoes, picked a peel from the table and tossed it in Willem's face. "You give birth to a baby the size of a *ochse,* and then you talk to me about weak."

Willem laughed and held up his hands in surrender. "*Nein.* That is woman's work too!"

John shook his head, a smile slowly spreading. These two. How they fought. How they loved. Sometimes it broke his heart. "I have been thinking," he said, his voice soft.

"Thinking? *Ja?*" Willem encouraged.

"I think I've asked everyone in Chicago. At first, people remembered. Thought they'd seen them but now…" He cleared his throat. "I don't know what to do."

Magda wiped her hands on her apron, the potatoes bubbling steadily behind her. "There comes a time, John. There comes a time when you have to… What is the word? When you have to let the bad go. You are a good man, and you need a good woman. Your woman was not good. She took your daughter, and there is nothing…" She scrunched her nose, struggling to find the words. "You maybe have reached the time when there is nothing left. So. This nothing. That is what is. Now, you make something with your life. You start, again."

Start again. He couldn't bear it.

"You become German!" Willem bellowed, trying, it seemed to lift the mood. "Bring him a beer, Magdalena! A beer for my German brother!"

John sipped the beer, not tasting it. He would give it one more week. He would have one more week of searching before he released the net. There wasn't anything in it anyway.

❧❧❧❧

"He's going to find me. He's going to find me, and he's going to slip his hands around my neck, and he's going to strangle me. He's going to strangle me dead." Cora stood at her room's window looking at Chicago burning. She was sure it was on fire, though it might have been from the factories, or maybe the orange of the trees turning. No. It was burning. If not now, then it was a premonition. She was having them all the time now, it seemed. She could feel John's hands around her neck. Closing, closing. A vise around her. He was always so cruel to her. So cruel!

"Cruel," she whispered. "He's going to find me and strangle my neck. Like a chicken. Like a…"

Something hit her in the back of the head. A book, tossed at her across the room. "If you don't shut up, I'm going to strangle you, myself. For fuck's sake, woman. Shut. The. Fuck. UP."

Cora rubbed the back of her head. Her hair was matted there and she could feel a goose egg bubbling. He'd hit her with a book! Oh, when she'd met Ray, he'd smiled like he was a god, but he was a demon just like the rest of them. He'd just hit her. Tossed a book across the room and hit her in the back of the head so she was bleeding. A book! She could feel the blood trickling and it made her angry. She spun on him. "You worthless…" She didn't have time to finish the curse. She leapt across the room. She was going to strangle *him*.

She straddled him on the bed, and she was going to tear out his eyes. Pluck them out like ripe berries. Only he was stronger than her, and he held her hands inches from his face and…he laughed at her.

He laughed.

"You are one crazy bitch, you know that, Cora? Do you?" His voice was butter soft, and she felt her anger dissipate. A soothed burn. She stopped trying to claw at him and leaned down and kissed him, instead.

"Don't go," she said. "Don't leave me."

"You're out of money, duchess," he said, as if he had no control over the situation, as if it was all her fault, but then he kissed her back.

She could make him stay. She didn't have any money left, and she couldn't take him to restaurants or the shows he liked. She couldn't buy him the fancy clothes like she had at first. But she could kiss him. She could shimmy out of her clothes and take him inside of her body and ride and ride and ride until he was soothed and calmed. An owned horse. She moved his big hands to cover her breasts, to grab them. "I'll find money. It's not all gone forever, just right now. Come on," she pleaded. She moved her hips the way he liked. Up and down over him. But he wasn't hard. He wasn't responding. That was the moment he pushed her off of him.

"Get off!" he said. "For fuck's sake, Cora!" He stood above her, and she trembled on the bed. She was a child, and he was her father screaming at her. "You're suffocating me! It was fun at first, Duchess. We had a grand time, didn't we? But it's over, now. It's time for me to find someone new. You're pure dried out." He said those evil, evil words with a smile as wide and bright as the first day she'd met him. And she knew. He'd never loved her. It was just because she'd had money. And now, her money was gone. He'd used all her money.

"Cheat," she breathed. "Cheat! Liar! Demon!"

Ray looked at her and shook his head. "Fucking crazy. It's been fun, duchess. But it's time to call it good, now. This is where I exit. You follow me or mess with me again, and I'll fucking kill you." He raised his hands and tipped an imaginary hat, then left. He left her there. On her bed. Alone. Again.

She ran back to the window to see if she could find him. If she could see him out there then he would feel the pull of her and come back. She did not see him. All she saw was Chicago burning, the bright red and orange flames growing bright in the night.

❧❧❧

Chicago was burning. Maybe it would be another Great Fire. A greater fire. The greatest. She wished for it. Cherry could see the fire out the window. She had no reaction to it. It just was. Mama Mabel told the girls to drink up, be merry. Forget the world outside. That was their job. But Cherry liked watching it burn.

Buttons was also aflame but it was a different kind of burning. "Samuel is coming tonight, Cherry!" she said, her cheeks bright with excitement. Samuel was part of their plan. Their Great Plan of Escape. Cherry knew that it was nothing more than a dream. They would not escape. You did not escape a place like this. This was hell. The proof was in the fire on the horizon. A factory, someone had said. Chester, maybe. A boy. Maybe this time, Chicago would end up useless as a matchstick. But Samuel was coming. Samuel. "He's going to marry me, Cherry," she'd told her, clasping her hands, eyes bright. "He's been saving money to pay off my debt to Mama Mabel. And then we'll get married, and I'll come back for you."

That was the plan. The Great Plan of Escape. If Cherry had any laughter left in her, she'd have laughed when Buttons told her. There were so many 'ifs' in that plan; it would be as useful as trying to put out the distant fire with handfuls of water. If Samuel saved enough money to pay off the debt. If Mama Mabel let her go. If he actually married Buttons. If Buttons came back for her.

It wasn't a plan. It was a dream.

"Cherry! My sweet!" The drunken man called to her. In the company of others, she was to call him Mr. Howard, but in the dark, when he stumbled with her into a room, when he did the things that men did, he told her to call him "Papa". It made her sick. "My little girl," he said, snuggling up behind her. She could feel him growing against her back. How she longed to be a Praying Mantis. To spin around, loom over him, and bite off his head with her mandibles. His body would stay standing for a moment or two, until the brain finally realized it was decapitated, and then he would collapse at her feet, in a heap. Then she'd consume him. He leaned down to whisper in her ear, "Papa wants you, my pet. Papa needs you."

She turned to him then, knowing Mama Mabel was watching and she lowered here eyes. "I have missed you, so," she said softly. Those were the words she spoke, but inside she said, *I will chew off your head.*

He grabbed her hand and pulled her away from the window, and the fires, and the flimsy belief that there was anything still alive outside of this place. By the time they reached a private room, Cherry had slipped out of her body and into a dark and quiet hole where she could wait, quietly, and make plans of her own.

❧24❧

By morning, the fire had been put out, but its thick smell still hung over the city in a dense fog. Snow was coming. You could feel it. John led the horses over quiet streets, lulled by the clomping of their hooves. He'd travelled these roads so many times now he didn't even need to lead the horses. They knew where to go. It was almost time to head to the stables, turn in his ledger and the money he'd collected, keeping a small percentage for his own pockets.

He, like the horses, moved by rote, almost as if he was disconnected from his body. The fog was thick. It reminded him of the silence before a storm rolled in. How wide the lake was, how clouds drifted over before the waves churned and tossed. It was that same quiet. The quiet of a monster about to awaken. The hairs on John's arms rose.

What made him take a second look at the little beggar boy? He'd seen him hundreds of times. He kept mostly to the same corner, though John had seen him occasionally on another corner. The boy never spoke. He just held out his hands and sometimes, maybe because of the boy's hollow eyes, people gave him things. A roll. A penny. A pencil. Why did John tell the horses to whoa—to stop? Why in the dense fog, did John pull over, hop out of the carriage and walk over to the boy? Maybe because with all of the fog, the boy appeared suddenly as if a lighthouse beam had fallen on him. Or maybe, it was because today, the boy sat with his back against the lamppost, not holding out his hands, no, but holding a book instead. John felt pulled to the boy, like a fish being reeled in, and he walked and then stopped to watch as the boy's hands flew over the book, furiously moving a pencil.

Something inside John shifted, the way the earth could slip beneath feet after a torrential rain, and his steps quickened. The book. *The book.* That was Lillian's book! "Boy!" he called. "Boy!" What he felt was excitement, but his voice boomed angrily in the empty street, startling the boy. The boy looked up but surely couldn't see John, not at first, and then the boy stood and ran.

John's heart banged against his ribcage. He could not lose the boy. There was so much fog, and the boy was fast and slippery, a silverfish. John ran after him, the boy slipping into the cloud of fog like he was at home there.

No, he thought. *No!*

He stood alone in the fog, a moat of space around him. He spun, trying to focus his ears. Someone laughed somewhere. Footsteps, a pair of them, somewhere else. A sliding sound, like a window being opened. The hiss of the gaslights in the last bit of dark before dawn. Surely the boy was there. Surely he could hear John. "The book!" He cried. "Do you know my daughter?" He called out to the emptiness. He yelled with all this might, "My daughter? Lillian!"

Silence all around. The sound of John's own labored breathing. And then...

The boy appeared in front of him like a ghost. He looked at John, cocked his head and then opened the book...

John collapsed to his knees in the street. The boy pointed to a picture of a girl drawn over the words in the book. Lillian stared back at him from the page. His girl. His heart. Held in front of him by a starving boy who, to John, looked like a savior.

ஜ௶ஜ௶ஜ௶

"Cherry! Cherry! Wake up!" It was Buttons, shaking her shoulder, trying to rouse Cherry from a deep slumber where, thankfully, she did not dream. In the dim morning light, the particulars of Buttons' face were blurred. Or maybe that was just sleep clinging to her.

"Are you all right?" Cherry asked, concern gripping her. This whole place could burn to the ground, and Cherry wouldn't care…except for Buttons.

"Oh! I am! I am more than all right! I'm lovely!" Buttons quickly covered her mouth, realizing, no doubt, how loud she was.

"Tell me!" Cherry whispered.

Buttons sat next to her on the bed, and Cherry sat up. She could see her clearly, now. Her auburn hair, normally secured on top of her head, was down and hung over her shoulders and down her back. Her cheeks were pink, nearly feverish and her breathing shallow.

"You're not sick are you?"

"If hope makes you sick, them I'm near death. He did it, Cherry! He did!"

"What did he do?" Cherry knew they were talking about Samuel, the man who claimed to love Buttons, but Cherry was still unsure if that was possible. If men ever felt that emotion at all. Everything they did told her otherwise.

"Samuel paid it! He paid the debt to Mama Mabel. Or nearly all. Two thousand dollars! We'll be poor as church mice, won't we, but I'll be free! And once I'm free, I'll come back for you. It's all happening! We're nearly free!"

Cherry tried to feel excitement. She tried to feel anything, really, but she couldn't. Every day, after every long night of her body being pummeled and licked and sometimes hit and scratched, Cherry felt less and less. Constant pain had dulled her body and spirit. But she remembered feeling love, and she tried to remind herself that she loved Buttons, and that Buttons was good. Something about what Buttons had said bothered her, though. "What do you mean he paid nearly all of it? Why are you still here? You should be gone and on your way to a church." Cherry forced her voice to be light and airy, the way that people did when they felt happy.

"Oh. Well, Samuel says it's a small issue, and he'll be back. He'd asked Mama Mabel for how much was owed on my debt and it was two thousand dollars, so Samuel sold everything he owned, and that's what he brought. When he gave it to Mama Mabel, she thanked him and asked where the other thirty dollars were. We forgot to figure in my room and board for this week. And for the doctor's visit. But don't worry. He's coming back tonight with the thirty dollars, and then it's done. Oh, isn't he wonderful? Isn't he a gift from God?"

Cherry looked at Buttons and nodded because it seemed like she should. Still, it was hard to feel hope for Buttons, and ultimately for herself. Thirty dollars was a lot of money for a man who'd sold everything. And what if Mama Mabel charged for today's room and board, too? Would she ever let her go? Cherry reached for her friend's hands and clasped them in her own. For a moment, they looked at each other, and Cherry thought she saw fear there, could feel fear in the slight tremble of her friend's hands. "It is wonderful," Cherry agreed. "You are nearly free."

"We are!" Buttons agreed and hugged her.

Cherry hugged her back. Buttons was as fragile and beautiful as a hummingbird, and Cherry worried at how easy it would be to for Mama Mabel to crush her.

There was nothing left for Cora to do. Nothing in the world left for her. Life was a hollowed out tree. A pit. She was trapped in a room that smelled of her landlord's sweat, his seed still sticky between her legs. Ray was gone. Zeke. John. What had she done so wrong in life to deserve this? Hadn't she been a good girl? Didn't she deserve white linen and silk and balls and someone to wait on her and clean the bat droppings from the attic? Why was she the maid, the whore?

The door to her room was left open, but it might as well have been locked. Her room, her life, was no better than a locked cell. She had no money. No food. She could rub her hands across her ribs and it was almost like running a stick across a fence, the click, click, click of her finger against her ribs.

All Cora had wanted, her entire life, was something good. Something pure. But it never happened, did it? She stood up in her room and began to pace. A caged animal, that's what she was. She had a funk about her, now. Maybe she was rotting. Maybe she was being punished. Being punished for being a girl, for surviving when her mother died. For being so pretty that her father couldn't resist his carnal urges. For lying to John about loving him. For leaving him. For loving Zeke and wanting him and feeling pleasure. A woman shouldn't feel pleasure, she thought. A woman shouldn't feel. She should have had more babies. She should have been happy being a mother and a wife and a cook and a maid. But she'd wanted more. She'd wanted...something of her own. Something more than the choices that she'd had. She hadn't really had any choices, at all.

She walked in a circle, over and over. Her foot was purple and infected, but she couldn't do anything about it. She couldn't even go to the streets anymore and lift her skirt for spare change. No one wanted to look at her. Her bottle of laudanum was empty and dry and there was no hope of getting more. The last time she'd tried, that evil dwarf had shooed her out of the store like she was a rat.

Maybe she was. "I'm a rat," she whispered, and it felt good to talk out loud. "I'm a rat-rat-rat." Lillian would think that funny, wouldn't she?

And then she stopped pacing. She looked around the room. Where was Lillian? Wouldn't she be back from the factory soon? Wouldn't she have eggs with her and a slice of ham and maybe some bread? Lillian was the only good thing that had ever come from Cora, and Lillian would take care of her, now. It was a daughter's duty to take care of her mother. Lillian would be back any minute. Cora ran to the window, and threw open the curtain, her breath cut short by hope.

She looked for Lillian's small form in the wave of shuffling people headed for work. The factories huffed in the distance as they always did. And then. Then, she saw her. Standing across the road looking up at her. A dark shape in the early dawning. "Hello," Cora cried and waved. "Hello!"

The person looked at her, and Cora stopped breathing. It wasn't Lillian, at all. It was Zeke. And he was crossing the road.

⋆⋆⋆⋆

In all of Chicago, The Packinghouse District was the worst. It smelled, he imagined, the way hell would. Of sulfur and death and decay. Zeke was ashamed of himself. He'd brought Cora and her girl to live here. Hooked her up with that Andersson. And why? Why such cruelty? Because it was fun. It was fun to make others suffer. To have that kind of power.

Now, of course, he was paying for it. That girl he'd held in his arms. Her broken and bleeding body. Something dark had seeped out of her and wiggled its way under his skin, burrowed under his fingernail and now wriggled in his blood. He could feel it there, twisting. Sometimes the surface of his skin rose and fell in tiny waves. It needed to come out, but the only way he could do it was to make amends. He'd tried to cut it out, had the open gashes on his arms and legs to prove it, but it was too slippery. Now there was an open sore on the side of his nose. The worms were wily. They needed to be charmed out. He knew this as well as he knew his name. And so he'd come here, to Cora's boarding house, where all his evil intent had drifted, then hung like a black cloud.

The house, itself, seemed sinister. The porch smelled of piss, and there was the low sound of crying in the hallway. Surely the sound came from some bereaved person, but it was possible the walls themselves wept.

He staggered a bit, but then righted himself. He could feel Cora pulling him to her. He had to set things right. He would set things right with her, and then her girl, and then all the girls in the house. And then he would set things right for Mabel and for him. He'd end them both, and then, finally, that wriggling beneath his skin would stop.

"I said, *Zeke*. Have you gone deaf already, you *dummkoph*?" Zeke turned to see Andersson standing just behind him. The smell of onions rolled over him, and Zeke's stomach turned. "You back, again? You got another filly for me? That last one is damned near used up. If she weren't still rolling over for me for the rent, I'd put her out on the street. And I will, too, if you have a replacement?" Andersson waggled his grey eyebrows. All the hair on his bald head must have escaped to his eyebrows, and Zeke held back a giggle.

"No, I don't have a replacement," he managed to say. The worms in his arms were waggling, too. He needed to find Cora, soon.

"Well, find me one! That Cora bitch is a nutcase. I should just throw her out." Andersson's chin shone, slick with some kind of grease.

Suddenly, Zeke had the man's throat in his hands. His hands were moving on their own, propelled, no doubt, by the worms. The worms spoke through him. "If you throw her out before I settle things, then I will disembowel you." He tightened his grip until Andersson's face began to purple. "I will disembowel you with my teeth. Do. You. Understand?"

Andersson seemed to try to nod and Zeke released him.

He was not followed up the two floors to Cora's room. He walked steadily and slowly, as if on a death march. The door to her apartment was wide open, and she stood in the middle of her room, staring ahead.

"It's you," she breathed when she saw him.

"I've come to make things right," he said, and for once, the worms stilled, sunk deeper into his muscle to give him some relief.

Cora opened her arms to him, and he fell into her sharp embrace.

❧25❧

Chester shoveled another spoonful of the thick porridge into his mouth. He wanted a big spoonful but had to take tiny bites. Without having a full tongue anymore, eating caused him trouble. But the porridge was warm and good and it slid down his throat like some kind of edible gold. He watched the adults, listened to them talk here and there, but mostly he concentrated on getting as much porridge into him as he could before they threw him out. He looked around the small kitchen, seeing if there was anything he could slip into his pockets and eat later. He had learned now to protect himself first. At all costs.

"You thinking of stealing something, you little urchin?" The man had a German accent, but Chester could understand him just fine. He shook his head and swallowed another spoonful.

"He is good boy, Willem. He will not steal from us. Not when we feed him, dah?" The woman, Magda, forced Chester to look at her and agree. She probably knew he was lying. Women, especially mothers, were good at that. Then she grabbed a roll and stuffed it into his pocket. "Just in case," she whispered to him, and Chester had to swallow real carefully, because that porridge was mighty thick in his throat.

The other man, John, flipped through Chester's book. The book that had been Cherry's...or Lillian's...or whoever you wanted to call her. With the pad of his fingertip, John followed the lines of Chester's drawings lovingly, and didn't that make Chester's chest puff up a little bit? One day, he would be so good at drawing, he'd draw the whole event of the explosion happening at the factory, and the men, and the killed workers, and all that he'd seen and burned into his memory. But he wasn't there, yet. Still, he was pretty good. Good enough that his picture of Cherry was making John's eyes teary. Men shouldn't cry, Chester knew, but maybe this was the kind of thing where it was okay.

"Is she alive?" John asked, and his voice was as soft as a spirit's.

Chester swallowed the porridge and thought about that answer. He hadn't seen her in a while but he thought...yes. She was probably alive. For what they had her doing, she'd be alive for a little while longer until she was all used up, and a man killed her, or she simply just stopped breathing. Cherry was probably alive. It was too much to hope the same was true for his sister. Chester looked at John square in the eyes and nodded, then he went back to his food.

"Do you know where she is? Can you tell me?" There was more excitement in his voice now, and Chester hated to disappoint him. This seemed like a good man. Not like his own father or the men at the factory. This was a man who was honorable. The kind of man Chester wanted to be some day. But Chester didn't know where she was. Not exactly where. He knew *about* where she was.

He held out his hand for the book and after a moment, John handed it to him. Chester grabbed the stub of the pencil in his pocket and flipped to a back page, one that just had words on it and he began to draw. The kitchen was quiet, save for their breathing and the sound of his scratching on the paper. After a few minutes,

Chester pushed the book back to John, who took it, looked at it, and his face immediately turned the color of an apple.

"What is this? What is this?" John shoved the book away. The man was angry and Chester was sorry for it, but what he'd drawn was the truth. He sketched a house and in front of the house stood a woman, her breasts bare, and her skirt lifted to show her fur. Chester didn't know the words for where she was, but he knew the pictures of it.

Willem took the book and studied it. At first he laughed, but then he sighed and looked at Chester. "You sure?" he asked, and Chester nodded. "This is not filth? This is true?" Chester nodded, again. Willem set down the book and placed his hand on John's shoulder. "I think the boy is telling you where your girl is. She is at a house. A house for men. A house in the Red Light area, John. You know the kind, *dah*?"

In his short life, Chester had seen a lot of sorrow. He'd seen men broken and beaten, and, like in the factory, he'd seen them killed. But there was something about watching this man's spirit seep out of him that hurt Chester right in his heart. It was the look of hope dying, and Chester hoped he'd forget that look, but he figured he probably wouldn't.

The German man turned to Chester. "Do you know the exact house?" Chester shook his head. "Do you have an idea?" Chester nodded. "Magda is right. You *are* a good boy. Give him some sausage. When you are full, we will start our search. The three of us. We will find your girl, John. We will make them pay for this."

۞۞۞

Mama Mabel looked at herself in the mirror. She turned from side to side and rubbed her meaty hands over the great slope of her bosom and the red, silk fabric of her new dress. She looked like a fucking red-breasted robin, didn't she? All puffed out. A mama bird just looking for worms to pluck from the earth and swallow whole.

The image made her smile.

Another day was wearily drawing to a close. The daytime was so depressing. Life was better in the dark. You could adjust the lighting, cover up flaws with heavy makeup. Cheap gold paint looked real in twilight. And everyone was drunk and happy. She wanted everyone to be happy. She really did. When her girls were happy they spread their legs willingly without making Mabel call in one of the guards to encourage the girl. To ply her open physically or with some snuff. Mabel hated to resort to that, to drugs. They were dirty, weren't they? But if they made a girl happy...well...that's what she'd do.

And she wanted the customers happy, too. Above all, let those pathetic little business men believe that they had shine. That they were important. That they were worth more than a wooden nickel. Make them think they were priceless, and they'd spread open their wallets, and the money would rain down, down, down, all over Mabel's heaving bosom. Truth be told, the house was doing so well that Mabel had more money than she knew what to do with. She'd installed a golden piano in the foyer and had hired a man to play raunchy, throbbing music, to fill the house with a beat to get the blood pumping, and those cocks good and hard and ready to spend their money. Mabel had lots and lots of money. She liked money. Money gave her the one thing she craved most of all. The thing that made *her* happy. Money gave her power.

She'd always had a thirst for it. Her sister had called her a vampire, sucking on people's fortunes. Controlling them. And Mabel had to agree. She liked it. She liked seeing someone pleading in front of her, of holding their livelihood and well being in the fleshy part of her palm, knowing she could give them joy or devastation. She'd controlled her sister for years, and then Sarah had gone off and done the unthinkable. She leapt, didn't she? Right off the roof of this house, and made sure that Mabel would watch her do it. Made sure to look her right in the eyes and say "It's all your fault, sister. You did this to me." But Mabel hadn't. Mabel managed Sarah, she took care of her, she made sure the men were clean and paid the right money. When Sarah had Zeke, Mabel had given them a private room when Sarah wasn't working. And Mabel had found other girls and there were more men and she'd managed it all and Sarah acted as if giving over her body was the worst thing. It wasn't. The worst thing was thinking it mattered.

She tried not to think about it. Sarah had made her own decisions. Mabel couldn't rescue someone that was bent on destroying themselves, even if they held her heart in their hand.

There was a knock on her door, and it slowly swung open. Mabel looked in the mirror and could see sweet, tentative, little Buttons approaching, holding the hand of that pathetic suitor of hers. Mabel smiled at her reflection. If she were a real vampire, she wouldn't have been able to see herself.

Still, she could pretend. Mama Mabel showed her fangs. She was about to have some fun.

❧❧❧

Cora clung to him, the way a bat clings to a tree and sometimes looks like a dead leaf rustling in the wind. He was here. She would be all right now, because Zeke was back, and he would love her, and she could go back to the way things were before.

"I've come to make things right," he said.

His breath warmed her ear and her shoulder, seeping into her skin that only moments ago had been so cold. Or hot. Maybe she was both things at once. Cora didn't know anymore. She made a sound that was either a laugh or a cry or something in between.

"How do I make it right, Cora?"

She pulled away from him, but only so she could look at him and see that he was real. He felt real. He was solid. He smelled like shaving cream. There was the old scar on the underside of his chin. The place where his auntie had slapped him so hard he fell and hit his chin on a table, splitting the skin. He'd been two or three at the time, but he said he still remembered it.. She touched it with her fingertips. It almost seemed to move under her fingers. She pulled away.

"Did you hear me, Cora? I've come to help. What can I do?"

She started to hum. Her mind was answering him, but her lips were humming. Can you make me sixteen again? Can you meet me before Lilliana swelled my stomach, before John got to me? Before my father crawled all over me? Before my mother died with my brother between her legs? Can you start everything over again? Can you make the world spin backwards, Zeke, because that's what I want.

"Backwards," she said. Really, it was more of a sigh. Words were troublesome things, lately. Words were roof tacks in her mouth.

"Backwards? I don't understand." He looked at her. He had brown eyes. Wooden eyes. Maybe he wasn't real, after all. "What's wrong with you? Are you…God. You're high aren't you? And you stink, Cora. You stink!"

And with that, she started to hit him. Over and over, but he held her arms.

"Calm down, little bird. Calm down. I'm sorry. I'm sorry!" He was gentle, again, and he held her to him, and she started to feel that maybe he could make things right. "I only meant…You smell wrong, Cora. You smell like something's wrong."

"Oh, I'm fine!" She sang. "I'm fine, fine, fine, now that you're here, and you've come to make things right." She was not fine. She knew that. She was rotting. There was something wrong with her foot. And maybe, sometimes, she thought, maybe there was something wrong with her mind.

"I'm sorry," he said again, and he kissed the top of her head.

Cora stilled. She *stilled*. It was such a simple thing, to be held. To be cared for. To have someone take the weight of living off your shoulders and hold it for you for a time. They began to sway as if a band was playing. Cora hummed. A band was playing, and it was summer, and there were stacks of hay to sit on, and there was tart lemonade, and she had raspberry jam and warm bread and a cherry pie in a contest, and Zeke was with her, and the world was all right and Lillian was safe.

"Oh," she said. "Lillian?" She said her daughter's name like it was a question, and maybe it was.

"Is that what you want? I can do that. I want to do that. I'm going to bring your daughter back to you, Cora. I can't bring the other one back…but…" he faltered and his voice had changed. Tightened somehow. "I'll bring her back to you, and then everything will be the way it should be, and I'll get some peace."

Cora nodded, swaying in his arms, and listened to the band. Someone was singing about having just a little piece, and wouldn't that be nice? To get what she deserved, for once.

❧26❧

BUTTONS

*I*t's over, isn't it? Buttons thought. She didn't think it would be, but it was, wasn't it? Samuel was gone, and Mama Mabel, the bitch, Mama Mabel was in her room getting fat off his money. *And, oh, God, Samuel. My Samuel. He's gone!*

Samuel had the money. He had the money in his hand and he gave it to Mama Mabel, all two thousand of it. Mama Mabel looked at Samuel and said "But it's two-thousand and thirty dollars, son. You forgot to factor in today's room and board, didn't you?" And Buttons knew then. She knew that Mama Mabel was pulling a fast one but she so wanted to believe. Samuel looked shiny. He said, "Of course," and then "I'll be back tomorrow," and Buttons had worried he wouldn't be. But then he had come back.

And he had the money, didn't he? And didn't he do just what he'd promised Buttons? Didn't he come with thirty dollars? He was bruised and his spirit broken, and he'd said, "Don't ask me how I got it, love." He called her love. Don't ask me, he'd said, and Buttons didn't, but she knew.

196

Didn't he steal it? That poor, sweet man who'd never done a single immoral thing in his life, except maybe walk in here that one night and meet Buttons. And hadn't Mama Mabel pushed him to cross some line within himself.

Buttons shook her head, trying to shake away the thoughts. But it was fate that brought us together and the dear lord above. Soul mates, we were, weren't we? Oh, god. Weren't we?

But then he came back, and he had the thirty dollars, and he was bruised and broken and he handed Mama Mabel the money, and they were almost there, Buttons was almost free, and they are almost married, and all of this was almost behind me, and Mama Mabel looked at him and she licked those red lips, those bloody lips and took the money from him with her claw and she said…

Buttons took a deep breath. The memory lodged in her throat like a chicken bone, sideways.

…Mama Mabel said "It's two thousand and thirty dollars. This is thirty. Where's the other two thousand?" And she smiled. The bitch! She *smiled*.

And Samuel said, "No, I gave you two thousand dollars, yesterday. There was just thirty dollars left! And now you have it. Buttons is mine!"

He reached for Buttons, then, didn't he? But Mama Mabel got to her first, and she said real soft like "I don't remember you paying for nothing yesterday. You weren't even here." It was the knife in the heart, that. Buttons felt it. Right here.

"I was here! I paid you! I did!" he cried, and Buttons looked at Mama Mabel, and Buttons knew. Mama Mabel had never intended to let her go, at all.

"You were never here," Mama Mabel said, her lips the red of Satan himself. "You never paid me a cent. Or you'd have a receipt. Wouldn't you?"

A demon slipped into the room then and sucked in all the air, and Buttons couldn't breathe, and Samuel, he shrunk. Right there in front of her, Samuel got smaller. And Buttons said, "No, Samuel! It's not true! I'm yours!"

Buttons' thoughts ran together, a whirlwind, a tornado. I'm his! I'm his! He's going to rescue me, and we will run from here, and we will get married, and then we'll be rich, and I'll come back for Cherry, I will, because I love her. And I'll even help Rose. Because that's what you do. You help people! You keep your word! Only...

Only.

Only Samuel didn't say anything. He didn't look at Buttons. He just walked out of the room, and Buttons ran to the window, and she pounded. She pounded until her hands were red as Mama Mabel's lips, and she kept pounding until Mama Mabel's laughter stopped her.

Buttons stopped and turned to look at Mama Mabel and Mama said, "A man will always let you down, honey. Let this be your lesson from Mama Mabel. Consider it a gift. Better to know it now while you're still young enough and pretty."

Buttons opened her mouth and screamed. And then she ran. Her thoughts echoing the pounding of her feet. She thought, *I am running. I am running for my freedom. For my life. For safety.*

"Samuel!" she shrieked. "Samuel!" And she made it out the door.

She thought, I am running and I can hear them running after me, Franz and Mama Mabel, maybe Zeke, but I am lightening fast, because I am free, and I am to the street and I can hear the horses coming, and I am free, I am free, I am fr—

∾27∾

herry knew the exact moment that she was transformed. It was the moment she heard Buttons crying, screaming, the moment she ran to her window, naked, old semen spilling from between her legs, and she looked out the window and saw Buttons running right into the road and the carriage coming at her. The moment that Cherry cracked was the same moment the carriage ran into Buttons, tossing her body through the air, her red hair catching a glimmer of sunshine as it spun.

Cherry cracked wide open then, and any remnants of Lillian seeped into the floor. She will never be Lillian, again. It is too late. She is lost to the underworld, now. But maybe Buttons, maybe Buttons is actually free.

She turned from the window. The man in the bed was hairy and naked. He was hard as a pole. He was confused. "What the…" he started, but she silenced him by climbing on top of him and impaling herself. She rode him furiously. She was not a girl, but an insect. It didn't hurt. Not anymore. Anything worth hurting left her moments ago.

❧28❧

There were two million people living in Chicago, and thousands of mansions, houses, apartments, and even shacks and tents in the Packinghouse District. But there was really only one area they needed to go to begin their search.

Willem turned the carriage away from the opulent greenery of The Grand Avenue, with its brick facades and lush lawns, and headed downtown to the Levee: the dusty Red Light District where bars and brothels sat arm and arm with gambling and opium dens. Dearborn Street nearly shook with excitement, as if it was a living thing. At night, the doors swung wide so golden light and piano music poured into the street. Smoke drifted through those doors as if the beast were breathing.

Any dark dream was possible in the Levee, if you had the cash.

Just two blocks long, it was the spine of desire.

John had taken many people here. Groups of men, drunken already, and looking for a fight, a fame, or a woman. Maybe looking for all of it at once. He'd drifted by the houses once, in the light, when things were quieter. Maybe he knew, deep down, that this was where Lillian had ended up. Maybe he didn't want to know.

Now, there was no escaping it. The boy had nodded as soon as they crossed 22nd Street. He knew too. His wide eyes seemed to say this was where the girl had gone.

Night was thickening, and already, women stood in those open doorways, half-dressed or completely naked. John tried not to look. But one of them could be his daughter. So he did look.

"Some nights, I do not mind dropping off the men here." Willem said, his words sharp and biting in the carriage. "But tonight," he admitted, "It is a little like looking at death."

"Come here, daddy!" a woman called to them. She was older than Lillian. Her breasts already weighted by the burden of bearing children, her hips wide and full. Her nipples, even in the shadows, seemed an angry purple. "Come give me a kiss!" She grabbed herself then, and John turned his head. Piano music trilled, and it made him sick to his stomach. The things that happened here. The things that were happening to Lillian. He could kill Cora. He really could. Gut her like a fish. One, smooth stroke.

John looked at the boy. The boy shook his head. This was not the place. He'd drawn a picture of a house, not one of these strips of homes or businesses or whatever they were.

"The Everleigh Club?" John asked, hopefully. He'd heard of it. It was an expensive place, for only the elite. But of all the horrors, that place would be a lesser evil. At least, they took care of their girls there. He so hoped she was cared for.

"The idea," Willem said. "Is *goot*." He urged the horses on.

The boy sat silently. Of course he did. He didn't have a tongue. The horror of that, too. The world was a cruel place, and John was witness to that. There was a story he'd read years ago. A Christmas story. With Scrooge and a young cripple boy. The boy reminded him of that character. That Tiny Tim.

"I need to call you something," John said. "Can I call you Tim?"

The boy nodded and smiled. And John saw him not as an urchin, just then, but a hungry boy who was missing his two front teeth. If they found his girl, John would do everything in his power to look after Tim. Maybe he'd do everything he could even if they didn't find her. They might not find her.

Then there was a grunting noise, a sort of choking. John realized it was Tim, and he was bouncing in his seat and pointing. He was pointing at a house just on the corner of 23rd and 24th, on the outer arm of the Levee District. It was a white two-story clapboard house with a wide front porch and two very strong looking men guarding the front doors.

The boy held up his book and the picture he'd drawn. It was the same house. The very same. All it was missing was the naked women.

John feared they would find plenty of naked women inside its doors. And one of them might be Lillian.

Willem stopped the horses at the curb. "You stay here, boy. You with the horses. We go in," Willem said. "Me and John. We bring your girl back."

He said it with such conviction that John believed it would be as easy as that. They would simply walk into the white house and take back his girl.

꽃꽃꽃

Chester stood on the corner where the German man told him. He wrapped his arms around the lamppost and clung to it. It felt good to hold onto something solid. He watched the men walk across the street and to the house.

They will never get in, Chester thought. They are good men, and they are in a bad place where bad things happen to good girls, and they will never make it.

Maybe, like at the factory, there will be another explosion. They set that off to make money, for insurance. And Chester saw three people explode right in front of him. Were their souls worth it?

Maybe there was something he could do.

Chester grunted. He wanted to call them to come back. Don't go! He'd say. She is as lost to you as the dead are lost to all of us. If you go, you will be dead, too.

But he could not give words to his thoughts. They were stuck inside him. Chester moaned. The world was a cruel place. Cruel and cold.

The lamppost was solid. He slumped to the ground, leaned his back against it, and did the only thing he could. He took out his book and pencil and he began to draw. He would draw it quickly, exactly the way he could see things happening. If he had a record of it, then he wouldn't need words to tell the police what went wrong.

Because he knew that things were going to go very wrong.

The crack of a gun just confirmed it.

❧❧❧

The man guarding the door was huge, with arms like slabs of meat. He was also German. At first, John thought Willem was going to clobber the man, crack his head open, and John was prepared to help. His daughter was in this house. He could feel it. He'd do anything he needed to. The fish scale knife he carried with him was small, but its serrated edge was one of the sharpest things he'd ever seen. He could gut any number of men who stood in his way. He did not need to. Willem did not clobber the man or engage him in a fight at all.

Spoke quietly to him. Quickly. And all in German. Their words sounded like a spell. The sharp edges clicking together to form a blade sharper than the one he carried. After a moment, both Willem and the huge man nodded. They shook. And the man stepped aside to let them in.

John walked into a dream. Or a nightmare. He walked into the fog of a storm approaching in the middle of the great lake, when you know that the Siren of the Lake is aching for you, calling you to enter her cold depths.

The piano music came as if through a tunnel, and then as if he were already underwater. He saw girls in varying degrees of undress. One with her breasts bare as a bearded man nestled between them, his laughter the hacking sound of the dead.

Another man pinned a woman to a wall as if she was a bug on display, her legs splayed, his black-suited body quivering and pulsing. John looked at her, but the woman did not look back. She was dead, too.

There was no sound now as they walked up the stairs. Willem seemed to know where to go. He shook John's shoulder and pointed. "There!" he said. "The blue room. Second one!" His words were thick as molasses. John did not understand. He moved slowly. His legs were wrapped in seaweed, and the lake was pulling him down, down, down. Maybe he died months ago. Maybe his ship sank in a storm and the fish had already claimed him as their own. Maybe it just took him this long to realize that all this time, he was no more than a ghost.

He pushed open the door and if he wasn't dead already, the site surely would have killed him.

Lillian.

His Lillian.

His little girl.

There she was.

But she was no longer his baby. She was something else.

She was naked and gyrating. Her tiny breasts barely there. Her mouth was open as if in a silent scream. Her teeth sharp in the dark.

As she moved over the man beneath her, John felt his breath sucked out of him. He heard a rustling sound and a pair of black metallic wings unfurled behind her. They stretched across the room, and the sound they made... The *sound*. Like metal and bones clicking together. The man beneath her groaned, but John did not know if it was from pleasure or horror.

And then...

She looked at him.

And screamed.

❦❦❦

She was a bat. A creature. Something subhuman. A demon.

She was his daughter.

John lifted her off the man and cradled her in his arms. He nodded to Willem, and as he turned to walk out the room with Lillian, his baby girl, his still lovely and sweet child shaking in his arms, he heard the satisfying crunch of bones as Willem bashed the man's face in.

John was not naturally a violent man. But this had gone long past nature.

❦❦❦

Fucking women, Mama Mabel thought. Fucking whores. They were all whores. Herself included. She took a swig of the absinthe, finishing off the last of the bitter green liquid. It was supposed to be a treat, tonight. Celebrating her victory over another foolish girl. That Irish lass. The fool. Mabel had taught her a lesson, and the money would keep rolling in. Everyone had learned a lesson, and great Mama Mabel was the all-powerful teacher. She'd been looking forward to her little ritual with this drink all day. The sugar, the cold water, the swirl, the drink. The oblivion.

None of it was satisfying. Not even the oblivion.

"Cheers to Buttons!" she cried, holding up her glass. And cheers to her sister and cheers to Ruby and Rose and Marybell and Anna and Sophie and Rachel and Kimberly and...

She drank again. She didn't have enough liquor to toast all the girls that had entered her house and then left their bodies behind. "Fucking hotel for the dead," she thought. Or maybe she said it out loud. Things were wobbly. She was slurring.

The world was slurring.

What she wanted was oblivion. She wanted quiet. She wanted to Not. Be. Bothered. Not with money or whores or stupid men and their variety of pricks. She wanted to just be left alone.

Her hands fumbled with the desk drawer and opened it. There was gun there for emergency situations. And wasn't this an emergency? She couldn't reach oblivion on her own. She needed a little help.

She put the gun to her temple. It took her a few tries, but at last she pulled the trigger.

⁂

Chester flipped a page and drew another scene and then another. First the house with the men, and then Willem talking closely to the giant with the gleaming head, and then the house again but it was longer this time, stretched out on the page, beginning to waver, like a watercolor running in the rain. His fingers flew over the page. Chester could see inside the house. He *was* inside the house. He'd become a bird flying in through an open window and into the parlor with the man being sucked on by a girl, the three women in the corner naked and laughing and drunk. The piano player grinning maniacally while his dark fingers flew up and down the keys, as if he was rubbing the spine of a dead girl stretched across his lap. Chester flew upstairs and saw Lillian, a beast, her wings unfurled like a giant beetle, a cockroach, a praying mantis. She was poised over a man about to chew off his head with her enormous mandibles. And in the next picture, she was tiny girl, swaddled in her father's arms. The next picture showed bones and blood and chewed meat and it made Chester's fingers bleed. The last picture was of the large woman with the red hair and two much makeup, slumped on a desk. She could have been dead, but Chester also drew four bullet holes in the side wall. A new one to match the older ones. By the time he started drawing the outside of the house again, there they were—just as they'd said.

Willem and John and his sister, Meg. No. Not his sister. Chester's sister was long gone and probably dead now or bloated with a child. No this was Lillian. But she might as well be his sister. Everyone else had transformed today, so why not Chester? Let this small girl be his little sister. And let Chester be Tim. Her younger brother, bold and strong. The boy who would watch out for her and love her no matter what. And let John be…let John be his papa. If he would have him.

They climbed into the carriage. Chester waited to see if he could go too or if he would have to chase after them, be Lillian's constant, secret shadow. John turned to him and said, "Tim?"

Tim, for that was his name now, nodded and jumped into the coach. Willem flicked the reigns, and the horses lurched forward. It was full dark, now, and the piano played happily in the smoky air, and people laughed and danced and fucked and fought as if nothing had happened. Nothing in their world had happened. But in Tim's…everything was different.

After a nod from John, Tim slipped his hand into the mound of gauzy fabric until he found her cold and fragile hand, her hand so thin it was like holding bones or a claw. He rubbed her hand with his thumb, telling her with all the words that he could not say: "You are home, now. You are my sister. I will watch out for you from now on. I love you, just as you are."

The carriage rocked and rocked and rocked. No one said a word.

❧29❧

What was there to do now, John thought, but move on? He watched his daughter slowly bring the spoonful of soup to her mouth and sip. She seemed to move as if propelled by his own wanting instead of any real desire to take care of herself. And what should he do? There was something dark in her eyes, now. Something dead. Something of rotten fish. He would not acknowledge it. To acknowledge darkness gave it power to grow and fester, and he would not do that. He would treat her as if nothing had changed, even if everything had.

"Lillian…" he said and touched the top of her head.

She flinched.

"I'm sorry," he said, and pulled away his hand. He must go gentle with her. She was as good as feral, right now. He must be gentle and coax his daughter back to him.

"You drink the milk," Magda said, setting a mug in front of his girl. "The soup will feed your body, but the milk will feed your soul. You drink. You get better. It is what we do."

John nodded. If only he could believe Magda. All Lillian needed was to drink, and her body and spirit would heal. But would John? Could he just take them home? Could they start over again in Traverse City, by the bay? Would he work at the fishery, again? Would Lillian walk to school with her friends, and come home and play, and run into his arms when he came home from work? And what about Cora? How could they go back to their old life if Cora, the most essential part of their family, was missing from it? How did they go on?

"You drink some, too," Magda said. "In fact, we all drink and then we decide what to do. There are choices, *ja*? There are always choices."

༮༮༮༮

She tried to eat her soup and drink her milk, but it roiled in her stomach, a turbulent lake. The world was not real, right now. She must be *in between*. In between the living and the dead, the real and the not real. Was she a girl or a beast? Was she Lillian or Cherry? Was that her father or was he a cockroach that had slipped into a man's skin? Was that Chester, back from the dead? His escape costing him his tongue and his voice? Or was he a boy that looked like Chester, but was really Tim?

Her head swam. She was spinning. The German man and woman seemed familiar to her. She remembered them from long ago, before she'd changed, when she was simply a girl. But how could she be here now? And where was Mother?

She began to retch, and the woman brought her a bucket to spew out her insides. Maybe she was poisoned, and once the poison left her, she could go back to being a girl and Lillian.

When she was done retching, the woman wiped her face with a warm cloth and told her to "shush, now, shush". This woman was a mother, but not *her* mother. That much she knew.

Her mother was in an apartment, laughing and dancing, spinning in the money that she'd received from selling her. Her mother was a poison. She could not go back to being Lillian and a girl until the poison was spewed out.

The words came of their own. They were not her own voice, but the voice of someone else. Someone younger than her and frailer. "I want to go home," she said in that small voice, so soft they almost didn't hear her.

She looked at them and blinked, her eyes wide, the blink slow and full. She tilted her head and heard her bones crack.

"But first, I want to tell Mother goodbye."

❧30❦

CHESTER

I don't really know anymore how old I am, but I know that I'm not no kid, anymore. And I also know that what kids fear, monsters and such, that shit is real. Monsters do exist. They look at you from behind the faces of men and women, and sometime you can't be sure it's a monster you're looking at. Sometimes that monster makes you love them, and maybe that's the worst kind. When that evil exists in a ma or a dad.

My ma died a long time ago, and so I never got to see for sure, but she's an angel, now. My dad…he started out normal maybe, but a monster crawled under his skin. Tore up his thumbnail maybe and slithered right under. I'm not sure it's how it happened, but that's how I've drawn it.

The foreman at the stockyard, he was a monster all along, but he wore another man's big smile. He made you want to trust him. To like him. That's what they do. Monsters are charming. But monsters will eat your face when you're not looking. Or they'll eat just your tongue which is maybe worse because then you look normal on the outside when you just ain't.

I've seen things. I know things. And what I know is that sure as cowshit stinks, that Cherry's mom is the worst kind of monster of all. The kind that has a child and throws that child out. The kind that only thinks of themselves. And it seems to me that a monster ought to be held responsible, and maybe I am strong enough to do it. So when Cherry says she wants to say goodbye, I tug on her sleeve. I will go with you I am saying, and Cherry looks at me. There is a cloud in her eyes. Some hint of darkness. But maybe I can stop that evil from slipping under her skin. Maybe we can be okay, her and me. Against the world.

No monster's going to take over me. I am as strong as steal. I just look like a kid. But really, I'm a knife.

I will go with you, I say to her with my eyes. And I will do what you can't to keep you safe.

❧31❧

It was the smell of something rotting that woke him, only Zeke wasn't sure if it was Cora and her festering foot or the worms wriggling under his skin. Cora's arm, draped across his naked torso, was heavy, weighted. The arm of a dead woman. Only her shallow panting let him know she was alive.

He lay in her bed and waited for it all to be over. What was the point of anything really? Of working hard and earning money? Of fucking? Of being fucked. Every day was just a repetition of the day before, with only minor details changing. Like all those girls and the misery he was responsible for. But what choice did he have? Auntie Mabel sent him out to lure the girls in, and he did that, didn't he? He followed directions. He was a good man. He did what he was told, and he was rewarded with a room in a house filled with willing mouths.

Willing mouths but empty souls.

The woman next to him was no different. He suddenly wanted her away from him. Her skin was leprous. Contagious. Why was he even here?

He lifted her arm off of him and scurried away from her.

He'd never had worms before. It was all her fault wasn't it? It wasn't him or his actions, at all. He wasn't responsible. Zeke was a good man. A good, good man who wanted only the purest of things.

And he could change nothing for Cora. She was alive, but barely. He could see her soul leaking out all over the place.

In the cool air, he thought he heard Auntie Mabel calling to him. She always called to him. Reeled him in. Made him do her bidding. But wasn't it nice to be needed? Wasn't it good to have a purpose?

He slipped on his clothes as quietly as possible. The only sound was the churning of the worms in his veins. But they quieted. They did. They quieted. They soothed. Every inch away from Cora soothed him.

He left her. There on the bed, the door and window wide open so the winter breeze could swirl in. Cool everything down. Left her there. All promises to her forgotten.

He couldn't change anything. He was a fool to think he could.

He'd go home to Auntie Mabel. He'd go home and go to sleep and tomorrow, he could start over all again.

The worms said it was true.

⁊▲⁊▲⁊▲

Snow. Heavy and thick. Mournful. Papa drove the carriage, and she and Chester snuggled for warmth. The sky was dark and smoky. A storm brewing kind of smoky. But this was one of those quiet winter storms. Out on Lake Michigan, the water would swell and twirl, but here in the city, everything just slipped into silence, save the clomping of the horses' hooves.

Lillian waited. Or was she Cherry still? Or was she someone new, entirely? She didn't know, and she didn't really care. She was here and alive and she held Chester's hand. If she had any feeling left in her, she might've felt a warm kind of love to have Papa with her and

Chester's small, sturdy hand in her own. But all she felt was cold. Metallic.

And the snow fell, hushing down from the grey sky. *Hushhushhush.* They were travelling through a cloud. Around them, the railcar houses, the brick buildings, even the road itself disappeared. There was nothing around them anymore. Not even the haze of a streetlight.

There was a pain in her gut.

A stabbing.

She looked down and she could almost see the umbilical cord that still connected to her mother, slippery and red with new life. Chester squeezed her hand then. Without any words at all, she knew what he was saying. He was saying *now*.

"Where do we go now?" Papa asked. "Where is the house?" He pulled the carriage to a stop and waited for her to answer, but instead, she slipped out of the carriage and into the swirl of white.

It swallowed her whole.

"Lillian!" she heard him cry. Over and over again. And maybe she felt something then. Regret? Maybe. But the pain in her stomach was stronger, a feeling that had a bitter taste, and though she couldn't see within the swirling white of snow falling, she grabbed the cord, its slick red covering her hands and she followed it, knowing it would lead her straight to Mother.

☙☙☙

How long did she stand at the open window, the snow swirling in, her hand placed on her abdomen, now barren. How long? Forever. Never. Cora floated. It was a relief, this feeling of being in between. So much of her life, she'd been a kind of Persephone, underground with the dead, or floating high above with the angels. Now, for once, she felt firmly rooted, this pain in her stomach, this cord somehow keeping her from drifting. *She's coming for me*, she thought. It didn't matter if it was Lillian, or her own mother, or death herself. She was coming, and soon this would all be over.

She dressed, slowly, and only partially. She was trying to prepare but she was very tired. If Cora could just hold on…she would be above the pain of her foot, the sorrow of her own wrecked body. She wouldn't have to struggle anymore with the wants and desires of men, but she could be firmly herself. What a burden to be a daughter, a wife, a mother.

For now, looking out the window, her skin chilled by the building storm, Cora was…

She was calm. She was healed. She was real.

She was enough.

32

LILLIAN

I run, and there is nothing else, just this pain in my gut. There is snow and ice beneath my feet, but I am a cockroach, scurrying. Mother is calling me home, and I am coming, I am coming, I am coming.

Everything else slips away. My clothes, gone. My skin, unzipped. I am naked, and there are no hands on me. No men with their sweat and purple cocks pushing into my tender center. Buttons and Chester tell me to go, to run, and I do. There is a cherry tree just in the distance. Its green boughs are heavy with red, and I cannot wait to climb into her branches and pluck the fruit from her arms and bite into the soft flesh, the juice red and tart-sweet.

I fly up the stairs, and it is so quiet, shush. So quiet. I am coming. Look at me! I am coming!

The door is open, and I fly in, and she is there, a white statue, staring at out the window.

I hold the umbilical cord out, and I say, "Mother". She turns and opens her arms, and I fly right into her embrace. All this time, all this running, all this wanting inside…I just wanted her to love me. To love me.

She holds me to her. Strong. Her arms wrapped around me, holding me, stroking my hair. And I start to cry. It burns, at first, but it's also a relief. I cry because I love her, and all I've ever wanted was for her to love me back.

Mother, I forgive you. I forgive you for everything. I understand now.

We're the same, you and me.

We're both girls.

You didn't know, did you? How to be a mother? How to be a woman. How to be yourself. But it's all okay, now, because you are holding me, and I can feel the love between us, and I am holding onto this cord that connects us.

Me to you.

You to me.

Only it's not a cord I'm holding. It's a knife. My father's knife. And it plunges into her as if I am slicing a pie.

༒ ༒ ༒

Cora

I have been such a fool. Such a fool. Such a fool. All this time, I have been running, trying to find the thing to center me, the man to support me, to lift me and make all the bad things go away. All this time, chasing something when if I had just slowed down, if I had just looked around me…I would've known. The only thing I need is in my arms. Lillian. My girl. I hold her close to me, and there is a pain in my stomach, a burning pain. It is the pain of loving her and having let her go.

But I can now.

I can let her go.

It's all right, I want to say. It's good. This is good. I was not made for this world in which a woman's worth is based on what a man will pay for her. I want to be sixteen, again. Ten. Six. A baby. I want to be a baby and swaddled and loved and I want no more from this world. It's all right. I love you. I love.

Lillian and I sink to the floor. I don't feel anything. Not anymore. And it's that not feeling, that absence, for once, of all the things that have hurt me in my life, that finally, at long last, allows me to do this one small thing. I smile.

Thank you, I breathe. Dear girl, thank you.

Lillian holds me.

I breathe. I breathe. And then I stop.

It is all right. This place, this not being, it's a relief.

It's a prayer.

A prayer answered.

AFTER

❧33❧

Chester heard it in the air. A hissing sound. An exhalation. A release. Only then did he point the real direction of where Lillian was with her Mother. He knew he'd given her enough time.

❧34❧

John tried not to notice the stench of the house as he raced up the stairs. He tried not to take in the details of the warped floors, the walls not lined up properly, the wallpaper that was pealing with its lines uneven.

He didn't question how he knew where to go, or how even though he ran with everything in him, he knew he would be too late.

There were things in life that were inevitable, like the crashing of a barge into an iceberg. You could see it happening, but once you saw it, it was already too late.

It was too late, years ago, even before Lillian was born.

And he knew, didn't he? He knew.

What he noticed was that his girl was holding a knife and she was covered in blood. And there was a woman at her feet. Not even a woman, anymore. Not his woman. Not his wife. Just a body.

"Lillian," he said. "Let's get you changed and then I'll take you out of here. There's nothing left to do now. Don't you have anything here to change into?" She pointed to a dress hanging on the door. There were two. He picked the one that looked more wholesome, even though it was caked with mud at the hem.

His daughter was shivering. He remembered when she was born and how she shivered then, too, her purplish skin still covered with her mother's blood. This too, was a kind of birth, and they could begin, again. "Put this on," he said and handed her the dress. "I will tend to…" He couldn't finish the sentence. He would tend to Cora? To her mother? To that shell of a body on the floor with her pale bosoms, the purple foot, the blood blossomed on her torso?

His daughter changed into a sad looking dress, the color of a dead fish washed up on shore. He swaddled her in a blanket and held him close to her. They could find the police, maybe. Tell someone? They could go back to that whorehouse where they'd kept her and find the man that had started it all. Maybe John could kill him. Then he and his daughter would be equals, and he could share the weight of her burden.

In the end, he decided it wasn't worth it.

Would anyone care about Cora lying on the floor like this?

Had anyone ever really cared about Cora, at all?

He had once. In the early days. But then, had he ever really known her? In all that time when she'd said she loved him, when she cared for Lillian, had she ever told the truth? What did it matter? It all led to here, to this.

Now…now he just felt cold.

"Come on, my Lil," he whispered. "It's over, now. It's over. It's time for us to go."

The boy was waiting for them at the carriage and helped Lillian inside. He grunted at John then showed him a scrap of paper with a sketch on it. It was the outside of the house he'd just come out of, only there were two differences. One was the house was in flames, great columns of flame licking up the side. The other was a ghostly shape looking out the window. The boy grunted again, holding out the picture as if in question. John nodded.

They waited.

Lillian shivered and John held her. Thee boy returned, and he let him take the reigns and drive them away. When they heard the crackling of the fire behind them, Lillian, at long last, stilled.

EPILOGUE

1914

TRAVERSE CITY, MICHIGAN

Chester and Cherry sat together high on top of the hill, though he was called Tim now, and she was his sister, Lilliana. A name that was a little more mature, a little more grown. The acres of cherry trees stretched out below them, the strip of the bay long and blue on the horizon. The sun was warm, and the air smelled slightly of fish. Lillian flipped through a book of chemistry, but she seemed not to read it. She handed it to him. "Draw something," she said.

He shook his head.

"Draw." This time she shoved it at him. He took the book in his hands and flipped through it until he came to a page that was half blank. He began to sketch. He was drawing a woman in a long dress, her hair piled on top of her head. Lillian watched the woman form beneath his skilled fingers. She was beautiful. Achingly so.

"Mother?" she asked him.

He shook his head.

With all his might he tried to say the word to make her understand. "You," he said. Without his tongue, it sounded like some other word.

Lillian looked at him, seeming to understand.

Every day, she grew more and more lovely, more and more like her mother. There was a restlessness in her eyes now that had never been there before. He was afraid for her. Of the things that were coming. He would never leave her.

She handed the book back to him.

"Let's go," she said. "Papa will be home soon with Magda and Willem, and we should make dinner."

They stood, and they walked down the green hill, through the cherry orchard and into their quiet farmhouse. It was an ugly world, but just for now, while they prepared a feast for their father and their friends visiting from Chicago, while they peeled potatoes and Lillian made the crust for an apple pie, for now, there was beauty. They held onto it as if it was a trembling butterfly in the palms of their hands, knowing at any moment, it would fly away.

THE END

NOTE

If you enjoyed this book, please, please, please, leave a review and tell a friend. Positive reviews will help Tanya sell and write more books. And if you enjoyed the writing style of *In The Garden Room*, please check out *Tunnel Vision And Other Stories* and *Synchronicity*. The story "Tunnel Vision" was the inspiration for this novel and *In The Garden Room* is, actually, a prequel to "Tunnel Vision". Find out how it all ties together.

ABOUT THE AUTHOR

Tanya Eby is a novelist and narrator and lives in Michigan with her tiki-obsessed husband and two quirky kiddos. Find out more about her work and her life by visiting her blog at www.tanyaeby.com/blog.

You can also find Tanya on all the social media outlets including:

 @Blunder_Woman

 www.facebook.com/TanyaEbyWriter